Murder in Erin's Glen

BOOK ONE IN THE ERIN'S GLEN MYSTERY SERIES

A.P. RYAN

Glenside Books

Copyright © 2024 by A.P. Ryan

All rights reserved. No part of this publication may be reproduced, distributed, or transmitted in any form or by any means, including photocopying, recording, or other electronic or mechanical methods, without the prior written permission of the publisher, except in the case of brief quotations embodied in critical reviews and certain other noncommercial uses permitted by copyright law. For permission requests, write to the publisher at Glenside Books, Devon, UK.

This is a work of fiction. Any similarities between characters and persons, living or dead, are unintentional and coincidental. Erin's Glen and many locations referred to in the book are fictitious. Some other places will be familiar, but time and imagination will have altered them.

Contents

1. Incomers — 1
2. Greasy Palms — 7
3. A Cold Chill — 11
4. Crafty Locals — 16
5. A Road to No Town — 21
6. An Exciting Announcement — 26
7. Settling In — 31
8. Suspicious Minds — 35
9. Absent Friends — 39
10. Unpleasant News — 43
11. Family Arguments — 48
12. The Craft of Conversation — 52
13. Late-Night Reflections — 59
14. A Chilling Discovery — 63

15.	Shock Waves	70
16.	Sharing Thoughts	74
17.	Questions	80
18.	Was it Love?	87
19.	An Elevated View	91
20.	Unwelcome News	95
21.	Back Stories	98
22.	A Riverside Discovery	102
23.	A Gloomy Day	106
24.	Taking Stock	110
25.	A Letter from Angel Hill	115
26.	A Visit to Angel Hill	120
27.	Curls and Clues	125
28.	Fishing for Clues	132
29.	Home is Where the Heart Is	137
30.	Pooling Ideas	145
31.	An IT Revolution	150
32.	Valedictions and Accusations	155
33.	Time for Truth	160
34.	M.A.M	164
35.	Rosie in a Jam	169
36.	Tying Up Loose Ends	173
37.	From the Mouths of Babes	178
38.	Nun on the Run	184

39. All's Well That Ends Well	187
40. The Big Parade	193

Chapter One

Incomers

Ireland, January 1990

Marie, a slightly built woman in her early forties, stepped back to view her window display better. Her calloused hands and aching back were evidence of the hard work she had put in over the past couple of weeks.

'You've done a grand job getting your bookshop going,' Jim Noonan called over from the other side of the street. He was busy cleaning the paintwork at the front of the traditional-style building that housed his bar – The Thatch. He shook out the rag he was using, brushed the front of his apron, and checked up and down the street for traffic. Jim strolled across the road to get a close-up of the new woman in town. He followed her through her shop door and into the interior of her bookish domain.

'How's life treating you in Erin's Glen then?' Jim asked breezily, his broad, freckled face creasing as he smiled warmly at Marie. His small blue eyes seemed to disappear into the fleshy folds of his face.

Jim paused for a moment as he assessed her outfit, which consisted of a hand-knitted waistcoat held closed by a substantial ornate ruby brooch and a flowing purple velvet skirt. A pair of laced-up high-topped boots completed her outfit.

The loud jingle of the shop bell distracted them both. It was Dan, the local guard, cycling through the high street as he finished his round for the night. He, too, was curious about the new proprietor of the shop that had lain idle for so long.

'All right, there, Jim?' The policeman eyed Jim shrewdly.

'Ah, sure, I'm like you, Dan; I just keep going!' Jim gave a gap-toothed grin and shrugged his meaty shoulders.

Dan then turned towards Marie and nodded briefly. Dan was old-school. He liked to know everyone in the small town, and doing his rounds on his bike was the best way to do that. He was a bit wary of Marie, the new girl from London, and was reserving judgment on whether her presence in the community would be positive.

Marie mumbled 'Good morning' and scuttled behind the counter, her high-heeled boots clicking on the stone flags.

Jim was intrigued by Marie and slightly disgruntled that his effusive charm was not working its usual magic. Under the steely eye of Dan, the policeman, Jim took his leave, 'I'll be seeing you.'

Dan and Marie watched Jim cross the road back to his chores at his bar, The Thatch. The Thatch was a double-fronted building. A wide, red front door opened onto a bar on the right and a little confectioners and newsagents on the left. Piles of newspapers tied up with string lay in the hallway, ready for circulation and sale that day.

'She's a tricky one, all right,' Jim murmured to himself as he resumed cleaning down the paintwork. He glanced up at the window above the bar; a shadow crossed the window – Sorcha, his wife, looking out across the street. Jim sighed, tutted, and continued his polishing job. 'Sure, I was only talking.' His sunny smile transformed into a sour frown.

After a brief introduction, Dan exited the shop and cycled up the winding, colourful high street of Erin's Glen. Marie stayed by the open door but, chilled by the east wind sweeping down the road, returned indoors quickly, hugging herself to get warm. Safely back inside her shop, Marie popped into her little kitchenette off from the serving area and put the kettle on. She had wanted to ask Jim about the name of his bar. It struck her as odd that a slated roof building should be called The Thatch. Oh well, that question could wait; there were more pressing matters to get on to, such as her next shot of caffeine. As she busied herself with the coffee preparations, she mused on her first few weeks here in Erin's Glen. She had taken on the lease of this old stationery shop while still in her London flat. Her life here contrasted sharply with her anonymous existence in the big city across the water. The lead-up to her eventual move had been a long one, a whole year.

But she had done it.

She had taken momentous steps to change her life and fill in the gaps. Somehow, despite all the action, she still felt lost and lonely. Marie took a deep breath and shrugged off the tight knot of anxiety. Moving to Erin's Glen had been a huge gamble, and she hoped it would pay off. She just needed to tread carefully and get to know the folks in this little town where everyone knew everyone else. The hissing and bubbling of the water boiling in the kettle broke into her reverie, and she sprang back into action, stirring her coffee as she looked around and focused on the next task.

'Onwards and upwards,' she murmured to herself.

As she looked around the shop, considering what to do next, she saw a little face squashed up against the lower part of the shop window.

'Look, Mammy, hearts!'

Marie could just about make out the excited words uttered by the little girl with a red bobble hat on, her voice distorted by her proximity to the outside of the window. Her face was blurred by the condensation her breath had created on the glass in the chilly air.

Encouraged by Marie's smile and shy wave, the little girl looked back at the woman she called Mammy.

'Can we go in? *Please!*' The woman nodded, for who could refuse such an innocent and enthralled request?

'Go on then, but just for a minute; you've got to get to school, young lady.'

Marie opened the door and smiled, but before she could utter a greeting, the woman got in first. 'Hello there. It's lovely to meet you properly at last.' Sensibly dressed in flat boots, jeans, a duffle coat and a bulky scarf, the woman thrust her hand out. Marie shook hands with her visitor as she continued, 'This nosey wee monkey is Roisin, and I'm Trish, Trish O'Hara.'

'Ah, from O'Hara's Hair and Beauty?' Marie queried.

Marie had noticed the brightly painted shopfront just a few doors up from her bookshop along the main street. Owing to the bright pastel hues of most of the buildings on the street, the locals referred to it as Rainbow Row.

'As I live and breathe,' Trish confirmed, her ruddy face smiling in delight beneath her thick mop of unruly chestnut curls. Trish patted her mop and commented, 'I know, look at the shape of me. There's no time to do my hair! It's like the builders being the scruffiest house on the street!'

'Look!' Trish's daughter, Roisin, produced a purple-haired doll for Marie's inspection. 'This is Sandra. She has purple hair, and it *grows!*' Roisin demonstrated the magically growing hair by turning a key in the doll's back.

Satisfied by Marie's awed delight at the doll's ability to grow her hair, Roisin walked around the shop's interior, looking up and around, captivated by the books, an assortment of coloured pens and paper and an array of Valentine's inspired displays. Marie had strung up strings of pink tulle flowers that encased fairy lights, sprinkled glittering confetti between the book displays and had little lanterns of various pastel hues that gave a soft glow to the wooden beams and rough plastered walls of the quaint little shop. Little Roisin strolled around, one hand gripping her doll and the other in her pocket, mesmerised by the enchanting items on display.

Trish took this opportunity to welcome Marie and congratulate her on her business acumen, '*You* don't miss a trick. You're ready for Valentine's with your decor and romances in the window. I've not even thought about it. It's usually a good time to drum up some business with the ladies coming in to get their hair done for a night out – or the hope of it anyway!'

As Roisin explored the shop, she looked shyly at Marie, intrigued by this lady who wore beautiful dresses and spoke strangely.

Noticing her daughter's curiosity, Trish commented, 'There's another one who doesn't miss a trick. Don't be staring, Roisin. It's rude!' With that, Trish tutted and carried on her conversation, lowering her voice a little to fill Marie in on some background information about the previous proprietor of the shop.

Marie learned that the previous owner of her bookshop, Will, was 'a grumpy old so and so.' Also, he'd been gone a long time. 'To be honest with you, I was glad to see the back of him!' Trish declared as she took Roisin by the hand and led her to the door. Marie had been listening intently, keen to learn more about the elusive Will. 'We'd best be getting on. I'll tell you a bit more about him next time I get a chance to pop in. No doubt we will see you again soon.' Roisin waved her doll at Marie as a farewell, and the cheerful mother and daughter duo carried on up the street.

Marie reflected on how happy they seemed. This took her back to thinking about her own mother. Quickly, her demeanour changed, her face falling into a sad reverie. But she had no time to travel too far down memory lane as the tinkle of the shop bell indicated that her next prospective customer of the day had arrived. Marie switched on her smile as she looked up to greet them. She stood stock still as she registered who it was.

Or instead, what it was.

Chapter Two

Greasy Palms

Dan carried on his bicycle after passing Jim and Marie on Rainbow Row. He surveyed the array of shops and cafes. The higgledy-piggledy assortment of colourful traditional buildings with brightly painted frontages had a cheerful charm that most tourists missed. This is because Erin's Glen was tucked away in a valley, off the beaten track and relatively inland. Most visitors headed for the coastal towns and big cities, so a massive influx of tourists left this little town undisturbed. Dan often thanked his lucky stars for his quiet policing career in this small community that was left pretty much to itself.

Despite being overlooked, Erin's Glen had many of the attributes of the other locations that attracted the summer crowds. Being a glen, it had a sheltered spot surrounded by lush green hills and, in the further distance – Slieve Cairn. Slieve Cairn being a magnificent mountain that could look green, brown, purple, or black depending on the time of year or day you saw it. A clear river, Abanculeen, ran through Erin's Glen, and at points around the town, you could stop to enjoy its ebb and flow out to the sea far beyond. The town's main street stretched from Kildora at the foot of the mountain down to the old stone, hump-backed bridge at the other end that took traffic over the river and on out of town.

This was the route Dan took today. He was cheered by the familiarity of the buildings, people, and geographical features that he had seen almost daily for the six decades of his life. As Dan left the town behind him, he cycled onto the outskirts of Erin's Glen. The brightly lit shops and cafes along the main street had provided some cheer, but this quickly evaporated as he cycled towards this belt of low-level buildings away from the quirky but cheerful town centre. The traditional stone buildings painted in various pastel colours gave way to flat-roofed industrial units and fences made of corrugated iron and rusty wire.

The harsh sound of a radio, at full volume, hit him as he turned into Flynn's Motors. He reminded himself that this was one final check before going home to hot tea, a hearty breakfast, and a good sleep.

He brought his bicycle to a halt just inside the yard of the premises by the garage doors. Dan didn't dismount but just leaned round and popped his head into the open doors of the garage. 'All right, boyo?' he called.

Sean Flynn, the young proprietor of the second-hand showroom and garage, came strolling out, wiping his hands as he grinned at the older policeman.

'No problems here, Dan.' Sean drawled in answer to Dan's question. The young man raised his head, cocking his dimpled chin, continuing to smile with an insolence that many would find unsettling.

Dan maintained a level gaze with Sean, one foot on a pedal, the other leg planted at an angle on the ground, indicating this was just a quick check-in.

Despite the cacophony of the radio blaring out in the background, a moment's heavy silence seemed to pass between them. Sean, tall, muscular with a shock of dark hair, met the older man's gaze and continued to smile, a lump of gum nestled inside his cheek.

'All right, so.' Dan nodded briefly and set off on the bike. Duty done, relieved to be on the way homeward. Dan looked back briefly as he pedalled away. He was aware of Sean still standing where he had left him, chewing slowly on his gum.

Sean Flynn stood in the yard amid the cars, watching Dan's broad, stocky figure moving side to side as he cycled steadily away. Sean continued wiping his hands more out of habit than necessity, watching Dan disappear out of sight. He turned back into the workshop. As he passed the radio, he slammed his fist on the off switch. An abrupt silence descended on the workshop.

In truth, Sean was more unsettled about the visit from Dan than he would like to admit. He didn't trust anyone in a uniform, least of all the local fuzz. Mending and selling second-hand cars to the locals wasn't the most lucrative business in such a small town, but Sean got by as best he could. He didn't like people asking questions or putting their noses into his business. It also unnerved him when new people were in town. He, too, had heard about the new woman from London.

Many years ago, there had been a fire at Flynn's Motors. An angry, resentful scowl passed over Sean's face as he recalled that time. He didn't like how the local police treated him – with suspicion – as if it was his fault the business had burned down all those years ago. Will, his father, had been in charge then. Sean bristled with anger at the thought of that time. As far as he saw it, his old man deserted him and the rest of the family. Sean was left to build the business independently, without a penny, as his skinflint father had not taken out any insurance.

Sean never totally understood how his dad could do this. He left his family behind for what? This mystery never ceased to bother Sean. It fuelled his rages and ate away at any trust or optimism he might have had.

As Sean strolled around the workshop. Lifting tools and examining them in a desultory manner, he considered his relationship with his absent father. The truth was they had never seen eye to eye. His father was old-fashioned and hard on Sean. Arguments and disagreements were almost daily in the Flynn household, and it only got worse after his mum passed away, and it was just Sean and his dad.

Now, just what did that old copper want? Dan was close to retirement and came across as an out-of-touch old codger, but Sean could see past this. Dan forgot nothing. He missed nothing and had feelers out across the town, across the county.

Sean threw down the tool he had picked up and withdrew into the warm, fusty interior of the cubicle he euphemistically called an office – old trade calendars and even older ripped and creased posters hung off the walls.

A sour look crossed Sean's lean face. He stroked his stubbled jaw with one hand as he sat down behind the untidy desk. With dark eyebrows knitted together, he considered what to do next.

Just then, the phone rang. Sean smiled as he greeted the caller. Things were looking up.

Chapter Three

A Cold Chill

Father Gerard Reid paced up and down, the Eircell mobile phone glued to his ear. The wind whipped at his long black coat as he strained to hear what his housekeeper and secretary, Rosie, said on the office phone.

'Yes, I'll be there as soon as I can, Father,' Rosie shouted back for the third time, her voice lost due to the howl of the wind.

Father Gerard rang off and put his cell phone back in his pocket. The priest was getting the hang of the new phone, and it was certainly helpful in tricky situations like today. He sighed when he thought of Rosie's difficulties with her cell phone, purchased with parish funds; it was a total waste of money that made him wince with shame. Rosie had not bonded with her new piece of tech. She either lost it in the depths of her vast handbag, forgot to recharge it or misplaced her glasses and complained that the numbers were too small, so their upgraded connection was rather one-sided.

'I'll have to drag that woman into the twentieth century, before the millennium at least,' he chuckled as he waited.

Father Gerard continued to pace up and down outside the front doors to The Carmelite Convent of Our Lady of the Immaculate Conception Girls' School. He had given up on his car. It always played up in the damp and cold, and that fellow Sean couldn't sort out the problem. Only one mechanic within a twenty-kilometre radius. One of the many drawbacks of living in a small town.

Another major drawback for Father Gerard was being the only priest in a much wider radius than twenty kilometres. He felt weary and defeated despite his efforts to give an upbeat, faith-filled message of hope at today's special assembly Mass. His car trouble seemed like one more setback sent to try him.

He looked down the driveway from the school, keen to glimpse Rosie's familiar face at the wheel of her little red car. As he waited outside the school doors, head bowed, and hands thrust deep in his pockets, he mused back over the morning. The school's principal, Miss McGrath, had been as brisk and efficient as ever. She appeared to be a steady beacon of inspiration and positivity. The more upbeat she was, the more he was aware of how this contrasted with his taciturn composure. He tried hard to be warm and smiley, but when he caught sight of himself in a mirror or dark window, he saw the downward scowl his face seemed to like to fall into. Despite his years of training, he felt ill at ease with teachers and schools. His years at school had been a mixed bag, all right.

He huddled down into his coat as the wind scuffed about the remaining dry leaves at his feet.

'For Lord's sake, come out of the cold, Father!' Deirdre, the cook's assistant, called out of a side door into the kitchen. Her voice was barely audible over the roar of the cold late January wind.

Father Gerard, relieved not to be bothered by any of the senior teaching staff at the school, nodded and ducked around the building and into the kitchen door.

The steamy warmth and smells of school lunch greeted him.

'Thanks, Deirdre,' he grinned gratefully. Despite his sixty years, he still felt somewhat intimidated by teachers and nuns and was more at home in the kitchen than in the principal's office.

'It's the least I can do, Father.' The cook's assistant twisted a tea towel nervously in her hands as she asked, 'Is your car playing up again?' Without waiting for a reply, she continued anxiously, 'I'm awful sorry that fella of mine couldn't sort it out for you.'

'Ach sure, never worry, Deirdre, it's not your fault. I'm sure he did his best.'

Deirdre nodded, eyes downcast. She was grateful for the priest's understanding but felt ashamed about her situation, living unmarried with a shady character like Sean Flynn. She knew that's how people in Erin's Glen thought of her. That's why she never darkened the church door, despite her affection for the paternal Father Gerard.

They both glanced out of the window as a red Mini screeched to a halt right outside the front doors to the school. Father Gerard had been relieved to escape the cold but was even more heartened now to see his faithful Rosie come to the rescue. Father Gerard pulled up the collar of his coat as Deirdre opened the door, the wind catching at her long, lank, fair hair. Father Gerard's secretary and housekeeper, Rosie, jumped out of the Mini. Wispy reddish, grey hair haloed around her head as she pushed her glasses back up her nose. She smiled warmly at this man she knew so well.

'Ah, Father, I got here as soon as I could. Sure, you must be chilled to the bone.'

A heavy tweed coat swamped Rosie's bony frame: her legs moved quickly like little twigs below its bulk. Her heavily made-up eyes, behind thick glasses, surveyed him with concern. She rested her hand on Father Gerard's arm, ushering him into the car with promises of hot tea and homemade scones once they returned to the presbytery.

Father Gerard was grateful to have Rosie's chatter wash over him; it was familiar and comforting. Her voice sounded like gravel, no doubt the husky edge resulted from the twenty a day she smoked in her youth. He tuned back into Rosie's conversation '…The phone was nowhere to be found. So, I looked everywhere, under the sofa, in my bag, under the bed, all the usual places and guess where it was?' Rosie was in full flow, detailing her recent problems keeping track of the new mobile phone.

'No idea, Rosie. Surprise me.' Father Gerard replied with a twinkle in his eye. He felt the vague low feeling from that morning dissipate as Rosie regaled him with her latest story of phone trouble.

'It was in his nibs' basket. The wee terror had pinched it. I know he's a clever dog, but using the mobile phone is pushing it, don't you think?' Rosie was referring to her chocolate-coloured spaniel, Ziggy. Ziggy evidently had more advanced technical skills than his mistress. Rosie shook her head and looked at Father Gerard, laughing at her dog's antics.

'D'you know what? He'd pressed a button and got the talking clock!' With this, Rosie let out a crackling laugh that would have curdled milk. While delivering the punchline of her story, the Mini skidded slightly on the icy road, which only made Rosie laugh all the harder. 'No chance of drifting off with me at the wheel!' Father Gerard managed to grin rather insincerely; he tried not to think how long Ziggy had been on the phone. It was parish funds paying for that account, after all. But it wasn't only the phone bill that worried him; these visits to the school always unsettled him, and today was no different.

Chapter Four

Crafty Locals

Marie took a moment to register who the figure was in her shop. In the gloom of the January morning, she could barely make out the dark, veiled silhouette.

'Ah, good morning to you! And welcome to Erin's Glen.'

Marie smiled and thanked the nun, who beamed at Marie.

'We are so delighted that the shop has been taken over. When poor old Will err, left, we thought it might go. I'm Sister Mary Joseph, by the way. You can call me Mary Jo, everyone else does!'

Marie opened and closed her mouth, but Sister Mary Joseph carried on, seemingly divinely oxygenated, as she did not take a breath.

'We don't want Erin's Glen being taken over by nail bars, fast food takeaways, and coffee shop chains like some of our neighbouring towns. We like it just the way it is. And, of course, it's so handy to pop into the shop to order books and pick up stationery supplies for the school.'

Mary Jo's eyes glittered like sapphires as she cast them around the shop's interior.

'You've done a wonderful job cheering the place up.' Mary Jo took in the array of healthy plants in terracotta pots and vintage teacups, teapots, and plates displayed along the shelving, interspersed with glowing lanterns and pretty fairy lights. The shop had taken on a cosy appeal that Will's taste in decor had lacked.

Marie jumped in surprise as Mary Jo suddenly clapped her hands together and exclaimed, 'Wonderful! You are organising a craft group! How inspired. Quite a few of us ladies in the town like to get together to share our talents and have a natter. Count me in.'

Mary Jo's glinty blue eyes were fixed on a poster sitting on the counter. Marie had been just about to pin it up after she had drank her coffee. The sign announced a craft evening each Wednesday. Anyone who wanted to bring their project to work on in a group was welcome.

Marie was slightly taken aback that nuns were allowed to do this. As if Mary Jo had read her mind, she gave a small laugh and continued, 'They do let me out for good behaviour, you know!'

'Oh, sorry.' Marie blushed slightly, feeling slightly ill at ease with a nun, even one as effusive as this one. 'It's just I don't know much about your lifestyle; er, I mean your way of life... I thought you would be praying in the evenings...' Marie trailed off uncertainly.

'Well, only three of us are in the convent house now. I'm the youngest.'

Mary Jo pushed a stray hair back under her veil. Marie found it difficult to work out what age she was. She could have been anywhere from forty-five to sixty. Without the reference of a hairstyle, street clothes, or make-up to date her, Mary Jo appeared almost ageless with her soft, glowing skin, bright blue eyes, and broad grin revealing straight white teeth.

Mary Jo continued, 'I have to make sure the older nuns have had their tea and are comfortable for the evening, and I'm a free agent. Well, there is a bit of praying too. We have evening prayers, but I'm usually free at 7 pm on a Wednesday evening, so count me in!'

Mary Jo's eyes then fixed on Marie's brightly patterned knitted waistcoat.

'You're a knitter then. Did you do that yourself?' she asked.

Marie blushed a little more.

'Yes, it gives me something to do in the evenings. And I need my warm clothes here! It's not far from London, but it feels colder!'

Mary Jo nodded, tucking away bits of information in her mind. There were few incomers to Erin's Glen, and she was intrigued by the addition, a youngish woman arriving here alone with no connections she knew of. Mary Jo wanted to find out more about her back story but didn't want to push too hard on this first meeting. So, she got back to business.

'Well, I'm delighted you are here, my dear. Now... what was it I came in for?'

Marie waited patiently as Mary Jo gathered her thoughts. As she did, her shrewd, kind eyes settled on a necklace Marie wore. It was a small silver pendant with a Celtic design. Mary Jo registered recognition, but just for a split second. The moment passed as she continued, 'I work part-time up at the girls' school. I teach Physical Education. I'm not very organised when ordering my resources, so I need to pick up a few bits for my classes this term that I forgot to put on my order at school... I've got a list here.'

Mary Jo dug around in a copious black leather bag she carried.

'Ah, here it is...'

As Mary Jo went through her list of stationery supplies, darting around the shop's interior and picking up what she needed, Marie had time to observe the nun. Her contact with nuns up until now had been limited, and she realised she knew truly little about their lifestyle. Mary Jo wore a long cream-coloured tunic with a heavy brown cloak over it. Some rosary beads dangled from a rope-like belt around her waist.

'Great! You've got Post-it notes; Will would never stock these, but I love them. They help keep me organised!' Mary Jo enjoyed a nice bit of stationery and was relishing her first visit to the refurbished shop. Mary Jo seemed as captivated by the shop and its content as her young visitor, Roisin, had been earlier.

Marie fingered her necklace as she waited. Despite Mary Jo's role as a nun, Marie now felt more at ease with Sister Mary Joseph and decided she would look forward to getting to know her better.

'And what about you, Mary Jo? Are you an incomer too, or are you local?' Marie ventured.

'Me? Oh goodness. I've lived here for... forever!' Mary Jo laughed. 'Erin's Glen, born and bred. I've got my spot picked up at the convent cemetery, where they will plant me, too.' Mary Jo smiled warmly. 'Erin's Glen can be difficult to settle into as an incomer.' She surveyed Marie, who looked so hopeful and a bit needy. 'Don't be put off by any of the gruff locals. Some of them get a bit territorial. I don't know why!' Mary Jo laughed and continued, 'We aren't a particular beauty spot. We aren't by the sea; the tourist board seems to overlook Erin's Glen completely, so the locals are used to having the place to themselves. It would be a different story if they were in Galway, Kerry, or other tourist spots around the country. But there you have it. We are a sleepy wee northwest town nestled in a tucked-away valley. There are no motorways nearby and no rail station. No wonder all the tourists bypass us. Although saying that, Mrs Blaney up at Blaney's B&B is doing all right; she's got a guest in there at the minute, at this time of year, so we attract some visitors. But Erin's Glen is just the way I like it: nice and quiet. But that doesn't mean I don't welcome new faces.'

Mary Jo paused and looked Marie in the eye. 'I'm so pleased you are here, my dear. And I'll tell my friend Rosie about this craft night right up her street. Do you know she has a whole room dedicated to her PHDs!'

Marie looked back quizzically.

'PHDs – Projects Half Done! She's a terrible one for picking up a craft and not finishing anything. Maybe being in a group will keep her on track. She gets distracted, you know. Always on the lookout for a bit of mystery! Although she doesn't need to look far, her new computer seems a complete mystery to her!' Mary Jo laughed heartily at her own jokes, eyes glistening with amusement.

'Ah, you'll love her, she's a case!'

Before packing her purchases, Mary Jo swept her warm gaze over Marie again and then busied herself, loading up her voluminous bag. Marie had the feeling Mary Jo didn't miss much.

'Well now, God willing, I'll see you next Wednesday evening with Rosie in tow. You take care, and it is lovely to have you with us.' With this last warm gush of enthusiastic welcome, Mary Jo swept out the door, her tiny feet in their plain black brogues trotting out briskly.

Marie followed the nun's figure as she passed the shop window outside, Mary Jo waving and smiling. Her voice called out a greeting merrily to another shop owner along the street.

'Well, if all my customers are as welcoming as that, I'll be all right in Erin's Glen,' Marie thought to herself. However, she couldn't shake off the thought that despite Mary Jo's effusive chatter, there was more to her than she let on. Much more.

Chapter Five

A Road to No Town

Sean leaned against his battered red Capri, dragging on a skinny roll-up. The short January day was coming to an end. The heavy grey fog of the morning had given way to a fierce east wind whipping through Erin's Glen. The stiff breeze tugged at Sean's long, dark hair, and he flicked it back as he heard some female laughter. He smirked at the gaggle of girls who had just spilled out of the school's front doors, giggling and nudging each other. Sean followed them with his eyes, maintaining his pose by the car. In their wake, Deirdre scuttled out of the school doors, pulling on her thin mac and trying to haul her bag onto her shoulder.

She scowled at Sean, 'I told you before, you shouldn't smoke in front of the children!'

Sean let out a loud guffaw. 'Children! I bet those 'children' could teach me a thing or two!'

'And you're late,' Deirdre mumbled resentfully as she got into the passenger seat.

Sean threw the butt of his cigarette into the gutter and slid into the driver's seat.

'The nuns don't like people smoking near the school. You'll get me into trouble. I'm only scared I'll lose my job, love. I don't mean to nag.'

Sean ignored Deirdre's attempt to appease him and kept his eyes on the road as he drove along in silence.

'You know how we need to be careful with money. I need to keep this job,' she continued.

'Deirdre, just zip it,' Sean hissed angrily. Money was a touchy topic.

For the rest of the journey home, Deirdre remained silent. Her few attempts at polite small talk were greeted with grunts or terse nods. With a sinking heart, she realised she had gone too far. She should just be grateful to have a lift home. Usually, she cycled home, but her bike was in the workshop being repaired. It was a second-hand bone shaker, but it was all they could afford.

Deirdre considered Sean's profile as he drove along. She tried to focus on the positives of their relationship but struggled to find any. The truth was she had no one else. She was a late child to a couple who had married late and died young. But sure, there is no point in getting maudlin, she thought to herself as they continued the journey home. You've just got to make the best of it.

Sean announced his plans for the evening once he considered Deirdre to have been punished enough by his silence, 'I'll be heading over to Shenanigans later tonight.' Shenanigans was frequented by the less upstanding characters in the town and the bar was notorious for late-night lock-ins and illicit poteen.

'Okay, love, I'll make the tea early,' Deirdre offered. Grateful to be spoken to.

'No need,' Sean returned. 'I'll get something at the bar. You sort yourself out.'

Deirdre slumped a little further down the passenger seat. Her sadness and disappointment were apparent on her pale face. In truth, she was surprised Sean was heading to the bar; he must have settled his bill and the subsequent feud he had had with Gerry, the owner of Shenanigans. They pulled up outside the shabby home they shared.

'And don't wait up,' Sean called over his shoulder, the wind tugging at his hair and jacket as he sprung out of the car.

Deirdre got out slowly and wearily. She stood uncertainly by the car door.

'Right, well, I'll be getting off.' Sean turned on his heel and strode down the road toward the high street.

Deirdre clenched her teeth and felt her nails dig into her palms as her hands made fists in her shabby mackintosh coat pocket. Tears of frustration, hurt and anger welled up in her eyes.

'Hello, love.'

Deirdre sprung round to see Rosie, Father Gerard's secretary, trot by briskly, walking her spaniel, Ziggy. She quickly tried to blink away the tears and switch on a smile.

'Hello there, Rosie. How are you doing?'

Rosie stopped abruptly and looked Deirdre in the face.

'I'm just grand. Out walking this scamp before we settle down for the evening. And what about you, love? Is that man of yours looking after you?'

'Ah, sure, he's just after giving me a lift home in the motor. We're great, thanks.'

Deirdre hoped she had put on a convincing show of domestic harmony, but Rosie wasn't fooled.

'Well. I'd best be getting on. I wouldn't say I like the look of those dark clouds rolling in. You take care, love. See you soon!'

Rosie patted Deirdre's arm affectionately and continued to walk spritely along, Ziggy pulling at the lead as always.

The black thundery clouds overhead mirrored Rosie's sense of foreboding about Deirdre and her boyfriend. Something wasn't right there. That Sean was a road to no town, and it was a cursed day the day Deirdre took up with him. Absorbed in these thoughts, Rosie ended up walking along Rainbow Row.

Just as Rosie was mulling over Deirdre's predicament, Ziggy suddenly lurched forward on the lead. Rosie had been so lost in thought that she hadn't noticed the unfamiliar figure appear out of The Thatch, walking towards them in a beautiful cream-coloured coat. To her horror, Ziggy had launched himself on the glamorous lady and besmirched her immaculate coat with muddy pawprints.

'Oh, I'm so sorry,' Rosie pulled Ziggy back and inspected the damage. 'I'll pay to get your coat drycleaned; I don't know what got into him.' Ziggy, now the picture of innocence, sat on the ground looking at the two women with wide eyes beneath his curly fringe.

The woman's tanned complexion contrasted with the paleness of her coat, as did her facial expression with her words, 'Please don't worry, it is nothing.' She brushed at the muddy prints with a look of disgust on her face, her brown eyes flashing with repressed anger. The stranger was carrying a large leather bag, which she hugged closely as she scowled at Ziggy. Rosie was confused by how this mysterious woman spoke – a curious mix of Spanish and Irish accents.

Rosie wanted to know where this stylish lady was from, 'Are you visiting Erin's Glen?'

The visitor confirmed that she was visiting with the intention of teaching Spanish at the school. The woman flicked back her black, glossy hair hanging loosely down her back. Rosie waited, hoping to get more information. The other woman sighed and gave her name: 'Isabella.'

'Nice to meet you, Isabella. I'm Rosie, and this is Ziggy,' Rosie's warm smile faded; it was clear that Isabella was keen to get away. So, seeing that Ziggy's charm was not working its magic on Isabella, Rosie said goodbye, apologising again. Isabella turned her back and carried on along the street. Rosie paused for a moment. She glanced into the bar through the opaque window. It was quiet in there, no sign of Jim or any customers. Rosie shook her head and continued her journey home.

Rosie turned the corner and was relieved to see the welcoming lights of her neat bungalow come into sight. She sighed with contentment as she opened her front door and shook off her heavy tweed coat.

'Just you and me, Ziggy.' Ziggy looked up adoringly at his owner. 'Now let's get your dinner sorted out,' Rose continued as Ziggy followed Rosie enthusiastically into the cosy kitchen filled with enticing smells of dinner for them both.

Rosie looked out anxiously from her kitchen window. Her face reflected in the dark glass of the window. 'That's an ill wind that will blow no good,' she mumbled to herself as she pulled down the window blind and turned back to her cheerful kitchen.

Chapter Six

An Exciting Announcement

The school hall of The Carmelite Covent of Our Lady of the Immaculate Conception Girls' School was filled with the usual morning hubbub. Even on this dull January morning, the girls' exuberance was irrepressible. They gathered in small groups of three or four, chatting incessantly. The bell that indicated it was time to get in line for assembly was about to go off. When it did, the girls would file into straight, silent lines across the hall, ready for morning assembly.

Although the school uniform consisted of a dark green pinafore, green blazer, white blouse, and striped tie, the teenagers were adept at putting their spin on the outfit. Many wore a fashionable grunge look, with socks hanging sloppily around their ankles, adopting long, scruffy hairstyles. A few sported white-washed denim bags. Some more daring girls tried to get away with short denim jackets, but these were usually scrunched up in their school bags before entering the school gates.

Miss McGrath, the school principal, took a tolerant view. Some of the older lay staff and many of the nuns were not happy about the slip in standards at the school, as they saw it. However, due to Miss McGrath's dignified and compassionate dealings with all the girls and staff, even her critics were sympathetic to her liberal approach.

As on most mornings, the principal stood elevated on the stage at the front of the hall. By the time the piercing sound of the bell had ended, the girls had duly assembled themselves into their year group lines. Now they stood, silent, all eyes fixed on their beloved head teacher.

Miss McGrath was petite and graceful. She was dressed in a conservative tweed skirt and heavy woollen sweater. A silver pendant around her neck glinted in the stage lights as she smiled at the girls lined up before her. The crow's feet and laughter lines that her smile revealed added warmth and humanity to her kind face.

The assembled youngsters and adults went through the usual morning ritual of prayers and a hymn. An intense silence then descended on the gathering. Everyone stood in the heat of the hall with expectant expressions.

'Well, girls, I know you were all sorely disappointed last year when we could not participate in the usual Erin's Glen festivities. You will remember that Miss Byrne, our music and drama teacher, was suddenly taken ill, and Mr Caldwell, our art teacher, was also out of action. Sadly, this meant that we did not have the staff to support our students to take part in the annual parade. However, this year, please God and all being well, I am happy to say...'

Girls with wide sparkling eyes, open-mouthed smiles, or hands cupped around their faces were excitedly turning, grinning at each other...

'...this year, Our Lady of the Immaculate Conception Girls' School will participate in the 1990 St Patrick's Day parade!'

At this, a cheer went up. Some girls jumped up and down, others hugged each other, and some clasped their hands together in a gesture of dramatic thanks.

The teachers shushed the girls, and all eyes returned to the principal. With order resumed, the girls were dismissed from the assembly and flocked off to their various morning lessons. An air of suppressed excitement continued. As the morning progressed, girls secretly planned costumes in their imaginations or sketched outfits while pretending to take notes in class. For others, their attention turned to the parties after the parade, with schemes to procure forbidden refreshments and ciggies already taking shape.

At 11 am, the bell went again, releasing pupils and staff for a twenty-minute break. Girls rushed to gather into their friendship clusters along the corridors and out into the playground. All were keen to discuss the exciting news of the morning.

The excitement was less palpable in the staff room. One after another, the teachers streamed into the untidy room, desperate for their caffeine fix to keep them going for the rest of the morning. The kettles hissed and bubbled as cups and mugs were pulled from cupboards and bags, ready to be filled with a warming brew.

After the initial clamour of morning greetings, the teachers slumped onto their chairs, grateful for a few minutes of peace. Just as quiet had descended, Mary Jo bounded into the staff room, bringing a blast of cold air. Dressed in a baggy black tracksuit, her rosy cheeks and glowing face indicated she had just returned from a Physical Education lesson.

'It's a great morning for a run, ladies! I've just been out with the Year 4s! I was glad to get them out; to be honest, it would have been a tricky morning in the classroom trying to hold their attention after the news this morning. Speaking of news…'

Mary Jo had grabbed a chocolate biscuit and plopped herself down between Miss Mc Grath and Deirdre; she carried on, 'Have you been into old Will's bookshop this week? It's open again under new ownership.'

Mary Jo went on to describe the new proprietor. This was met with some interest. Erin's Glen attracted few new inhabitants, and the teachers were intrigued by the incomer from London.

Miss Byrne, the drama teacher, piped up, 'Erin's Glen seems to be quite the hot spot for visitors. I see a lady from Spain staying at Mrs Blaney's place.'

This snippet of news was greeted with mild interest – a visitor just passing through. The new resident at the bookshop remained the focal point.

With some enthusiasm, Mary Jo shared Marie's invitation to the craft group.

'What do you say?' She looked around her brightly, but the staff seemed slightly jaded and not up for an evening commitment in January.

Mary Jo noted that Miss McGrath fingered her pendant nervously and remained non-committal. This struck Mary Jo as being slightly out of character. However, little Deirdre said she would be interested.

'Great stuff,' Mary Jo enthused. 'I know you love your crochet, and maybe you could bring some of your delicious cakes too?'

When the bell rang, cutting short Mary Jo's efforts to round up a posse for the craft group, she sighed happily. She was delighted that Deirdre, usually timid and quiet, had volunteered to do something fun for herself.

'It's been a smashing morning,' Mary Jo mused with some contentment. However, a frown passed over Mary Jo's face like a shadow. Something vague and unnamed nagged at her—something not right that she couldn't quite put her finger on.

She took a deep breath, straightened her tracksuit top, pulled up her joggers and tidied away her hair under her bandana, ready to tackle the Year 3 camogie lesson.

Chapter Seven

Settling In

The darkness of the January evening closed in mid-afternoon. A few hardy seagulls swooped along the high street, driven a long way in from the coast by enticing smells and food scraps in town. Marie liked hearing the sounds of life on the road as she hummed to herself, arranging books, dusting, and replenishing stock.

The shop had been open an entire week, and Marie had settled into a comfortable routine, relieved to have the shop up and running. The tinkle of the shop bell broke into her reverie.

'Hello there, Marie! It is Marie, isn't it?' Jim Noonan's fleshy face broke into a grin.

In a split second it took Marie to answer him, he had swept his gaze over her and around the shop. His smile stayed fixed.

'Yes, that's right, and you're Jim from The Thatch across the road. I remember we briefly met the other day. How are you doing?' Marie put her hand out, feeling braver now in this friendly community.

'I'm doing just grand, thanks for asking.' Jim shook her hand too vigorously and continued, 'I've just popped in for an account book; I've lost the last one. Not my strong point, keeping up the old accounts.' Jim laughed as he rubbed his hands together. 'Don't let on to the tax man!'

Marie busied herself by fetching the required item of stationery, slightly bemused by Jim's open admission of his financial shortcomings.

A bit at a loss as to how to continue the conversation, Marie pointed to her poster. 'I'm hosting a craft evening in the shop on Wednesday evenings.'

'Ah, not my thing,' Jim frowned, looking somewhat perplexed.

'I was thinking of your wife... er?' Marie trailed off, realising she didn't know her name.

'Sorcha,' Jim offered. 'No, she wouldn't be interested.'

Marie rang up the till with the conversation shut down, and Jim approached the door.

'Oh, I've just remembered, I think I've got some post belonging to you. It just arrived this morning.'

Marie darted into the back of the shop to retrieve the bundle of post. She leafed through a thick pile of letters and handed one to Jim.

'From abroad, I think. How exciting!' Marie's attempt at a friendly remark was met with a sudden change in Jim's demeanour. The jovial bonhomie had gone, and he snatched the letter and exited the shop without a word of thanks. He strode across the road to The Thatch, the accounts book tucked under his beefy arm and letter in hand.

There was no time to reflect on this encounter as no sooner was Jim out the door than Mary Jo swept in with her usual exuberance.

'Ah, great, you're still open.' Mary Jo seemed to sparkle despite being back in her usual cream habit and veil.

'I've been telling a few of the ladies in school about your craft evening. Already I've got Deirdre lined up, which is amazing!'

Marie was not totally sure of the significance of this news and was a bit underwhelmed by the list of one. As she considered the report, Mary Jo carried on.

'I know it's just Deirdre, but she is such a timid wee thing; I can't tell you how delighted I am that your brilliant idea has appealed to her. You're an absolute star.'

What amazed Marie most was Mary Jo's ability to make a rather urbane idea sound so inspired. But she was enjoying the praise, having a sense of how the girls at the school must feel in the warm gaze of this remarkable woman.

'Well, I won't keep you, dear; I'm sure you have a million things to do.'

With this farewell, Mary Jo, her long brown coat in her wake, whisked back out the door and onto the dark street.

Marie strode towards the closed door and turned the sign from 'open' to 'closed'. The sound of the gulls screeching in the street had subsided but was replaced by some gentle mewing. Marie opened the door and looked down. She was greeted by a small black and white cat with eyes glowing green at her in the darkness. Before Marie had time to react, the lithe feline darted around her ankles and into the back of the shop, through the curtain and behind the counter.

Too late to shoo the cat back out, Marie locked up. There was no sign of the cat as she approached the area behind the counter.

Just as she was reaching up to pull across the top bolt, Marie caught sight of a female figure looking out the window above The Thatch, directly opposite her shop.

Sorcha, Marie assumed. Just as quickly as she appeared, Sorcha darted away from the window. The curtains were pulled closed. Marie was intrigued by this elusive woman and hesitated momentarily by her locked glass door. The street was quiet now, the brightly painted buildings and shopfronts a more subdued hue in the early evening light. The outline of Jim Noonan's bulky frame was visible through the opaque window of the bar. A small group of older men wrapped in heavy overcoats entered The Thatch. Presumably for a swift pint before going home for their tea. The activity in the bar below the room Sorcha inhabited contrasted with the blank look of the curtained window above.

'Now. Where are you, puss?' Marie murmured to herself as she moved across the shop and up the stairs.

The fluffy intruder must have skipped quietly upstairs. Marie took one last look around the shop, switched off the lights and padded upstairs, suddenly feeling weary. When she got upstairs to her homely little abode, her heart lifted at the sight of her furry visitor. The cat had perched himself on the rug in front of the wood burner and sat, blinking at her expectantly with inscrutable amber-green eyes.

'Well, you're making yourself at home already, aren't you? You cheeky puss.' Marie knelt on the rug and gently stroked his head. Marie's attention elicited a contented, rumbling purr as the silky-haired feline leaned into Marie. Marie pondered on her day, lulled by the gentle rhythm of stroking the cat, the soothing vibration of his purr, and the fire's warmth. A feeling of contentment washed over her as she realised she was settling into the community and getting to know the locals.

Marie *was* getting to know the locals but had much more to uncover.

Much more.

Chapter Eight

Suspicious Minds

Shortly after Marie locked up for the evening, Dan, the local guard, cycled up the high street, making his first round of the town for the evening. His dark silhouette on the bike contrasted with the pastel shades of the shopfronts and town buildings. The street was quiet on this cold evening. However, Dan seemed immune to the biting wind that tore along the road – decades of life outdoors, first as a farmer's son, then out on his beats, had hardened him. But Dan's soft heart contrasted with his hardy exterior. Not that he'd let on to anyone. He deliberately cultivated a brusque but cheerful demeanour.

'Don't want the local crooks thinking I'm a walkover,' he would remind himself if he felt he was coming across as a softie.

But he felt concerned about the more vulnerable residents in the town, which had been home to him all his life. He knew pretty much everyone by name, and the ones he didn't know or didn't see very often were a worry to him. He would constantly scan the shops and houses with their locked doors and dark windows, wondering what was happening behind closed doors.

And this evening was no different. He slowed on the bike, took a foot off a pedal, and stopped outside The Thatch. The usual rumble of conversation was punctuated by raucous laughter from inside the bar. He saw Jim inside, behind the bar, polishing glasses and laughing with the locals. The publican looked very much at home behind his bar, with his gleaming golf trophies on display. Despite Jim's less-than-athletic figure, he was a keen and proficient golfer and went to the local course whenever possible. Jim turned towards the window and caught the policeman's eye for a second. The smile on Dan's face disappeared for a brief moment. The policeman scanned the faces of the small crowd gathered around the bar; he knew them all by name. One female figure sat apart from them by the window, slowly drinking a small glass of Guinness and watching the crowd at the bar. Jim lumbered around the bar and came to the front door of the public house, the smile reinstated.

'All right there, Dan?' he called out, his towel and glass still in his hands. 'It's fearful cold tonight; I don't envy you on that bike. Are you coming indoors for a warmer?'

Dan let a moment pass until he answered, surveying the publican with a mild distaste he didn't need to fake.

'No, no, sure, I'm on duty, man. Just stopping by to make sure everything is in order.'

Jim nodded. 'Oh aye, no worries.' He hesitated, glanced at Dan sideways and then turned on his heel. The older man's scrutiny discomfited him. 'I'll head back to the lads then. I'll be seeing you.'

Dan watched Jim return to the bar. He angled back more as he stood, one leg still over the bike. He cast one last look over the front of the building that housed The Thatch. He hadn't seen Sorcha, Jim's wife, out and about for quite some time. He worried about her. He didn't trust Jim Noonan as far as he could throw him, 'And I wouldn't be able to throw his lardy arse very far.' He chuckled to himself as he pushed back onto the bike and continued to cycle down the road back to the relative warmth of his station up at the other end of town.

He impulsively turned off and double-backed on himself along Scanlan Street, where Deirdre and Sean lived. He slowed as he passed a low two-storey building with flaking grey-white paint. Another worry was that wee Deirdre, who had shacked up with Sean. With the intuition of a seasoned copper, he knew things weren't right behind doors in that household. He kept a steady gaze as he passed the run-down-looking house, pulled down his cap, and headed back into the wind, looking forward to a warming brew when he got to the station.

Inside the tiny house on Scanlon Street, Deirdre darted about anxiously. She had been out the back, calling for Patch, but there was no sign. Deirdre could tell that her worried behaviour and fussing were irritating Sean, who was watching football on a small portable black and white television.

'What's up with you?' he called over his shoulder before taking another slurp of lager from the can he had by the side of his ripped armchair.

Deirdre didn't want to make a fuss. She knew Sean couldn't stand her little pet cat, and she was reluctant to create a scene about where he might have gone.

When she didn't answer, Sean sat up and turned around to look at her. Deirdre stood, twisting her hands together, uncertain about what to do or say to avoid making Sean angry with her.

'You are so pathetic.' Sean turned down the corners of his mouth and glanced at her with disdain. He looked back at the television without another word.

Deirdre's heart sank, and she felt tears prickle in her eyes. She pulled her stained dressing gown tighter around her narrow frame and shuffled back into the kitchen. Sean wasn't an 'animal person' and complained bitterly about the cat's effect on his allergies. She had caught him before chasing the cat outside with a sweeping brush.

She returned to her baking. Making cakes and bread helped her ease the constant tensions she felt. But tonight, even the kneading and rolling wasn't helping lift the worry about her precious Patch. She lifted the heavy wooden rolling pin with one hand, rubbing her other hand up and down its powdery surface, dusty with flour. Just what had Sean done this time? And where was Patch? A hot knot of anger was starting to form low in her belly. She gritted her teeth, sighed, and stood by the curtainless window.

Deirdre's pale face was reflected in the dark glass as she looked out anxiously into the night, casting a distrustful glance back at Sean. She just never knew what he was up to.

And with that, Deirdre thumped the rolling pin down heavily onto the flat square of pastry with a thud, releasing a fine flour spray. Deirdre wiped the dusting of flour away and sighed deeply.

Chapter Nine

Absent Friends

Rosie was curled up on a comfy seat attached to a table that housed the telephone in the hallway of her home. Rosie liked to refer to this square-shaped entrance to her home as a 'vestibule'. Mary Jo had teased Rosie gently about her grandiosity, but Rosie's defence was that this was due to the influence of her late mother, who appreciated a bit of class. Rosie was snuggled up in a thick, fluffy dressing gown and settled down happily for a chat with her friend, Mary Jo.

The door opposite her opened into the lounge, and Rosie could watch Ziggy and the crackling fire as she chatted on the phone. The warmth from the lounge drifted out to the hallway. Rosie had resisted getting central heating put in and relied on the fire in the lounge and the range in the kitchen to heat the bungalow.

As Rosie greeted Mary Jo on the telephone, Ziggy, roused from his slumbers in his basket, sat bolt upright with a quizzical expression on his chocolate-coloured face. After a moment, he decided to investigate further, padded out to see what she was up to, and looked up appealingly. Rosie sat upright and patted her lap, allowing him to leap up, which he did eagerly.

'Sorry, Mary Jo, that's just Ziggy looking for attention again. You'd think I never gave him a kind look the way he gets on with those big sad eyes.'

Rosie bent down and nestled her face into his thick fur. Her voice was muffled long enough for Mary Jo to jump in with her next piece of news.

'Have you been into the new stationers yet, Rosie?' Without waiting for an answer, Mary Jo went on. 'It's been taken over by a lovely girl, over from London. She's done a grand job doing the place up, dragging it into the twentieth century! Old Will had let it run down before he disappeared off. I'm delighted to see the shop get a new lease of life after all those years lying idle.'

Rosie was curious about the legalities of selling the leasehold on the shop. She was just about to open her mouth to comment on this when Mary Jo continued to share the news about the craft group and how she had got Deirdre to go.

Before they rang off, Mary Jo had secured Rosie's agreement to attend the craft group, and they had mused on the possibility of using some of the group's time to create St Patrick's themed crafts for the parade in March. Rosie was always looking for ways to raise funds for the new church building, and this was a great opportunity.

Rosie was about to say goodbye when Mary Jo asked her if she had recently seen Miss McGrath to talk to. Despite Mary Jo's casual attitude to her own personal address, she always referred to her principal by her formal title and surname. Rosie and Mairead McGrath had known each other for most of their lives, and in contrast to Mary

Jo, she usually referred to the school head by her first name. Rosie considered the question.

'Come to think of it – no. I haven't seen Mairead McGrath properly since just after Christmas.' Rosie paused to think about exactly when she had seen her; 'I've seen her at Mass on Sundays, but she's had to rush off, not staying for coffee as usual. I thought nothing of it as she was so busy with schoolwork. She also has her mother to take care of. I don't know how she does it all. Do you ask for any particular reason?' Rosie queried.

'I don't know, Rosie; she hasn't been herself lately. She refused point blank to go to the craft group. I know she's busy, but even head teachers need a night off occasionally. Maybe she is just working too hard. You know how conscientious she is.'

Rosie did know. Mary Jo's observations about her long-time acquaintance worried her. Mairead McGrath was usually an active member of the community. Her absence disturbed Rosie. There was something very unsettling in the air recently, and Rosie kept her ears and eyes open.

'Oh, before you go, Mary Jo, what's that new girl's name? The girl who has taken over Will's place?'

'Marie, Marie Miller, I believe.'

Rosie looked thoughtful but shook her head. 'Ah, right, thanks, Mary Jo. Well, I look forward to meeting her.'

The friends said goodnight, God bless and rang off.

'We'll get to the bottom of this, Ziggy, won't we?' Rosie ruffled Ziggy's soft, silky fur as he looked up at her earnestly, giving a short bark of agreement.

Rosie spent the rest of the evening sorting through her craft basket, choosing supplies for next week's get-together. Rosie had set up the craft room in her house while caring for her elderly mother. Knitting, sewing, or crocheting had given her something to do in the evenings when she was confined at home due to the need to be available for caring duties. In addition, having a project to focus on helped her deal with the vast void her mother's death had opened up. Being a practical sort, Rosie did her best to shake off her sad mood and focused on untangling balls of wool and folding squares of fabric. The gentle tasks soothed her tonight, but as she switched off the lights that night, she couldn't shake off the unease that had been building over the past few weeks.

The telephone lines were buzzing that night in Erin's Glen. Just up the road on the high street, Jim Noonan was having an intense, hushed conversation in the back lobby of the bar. It was a weeknight, and business was slow, especially in January. He couldn't hear Sorcha moving about upstairs, so he had taken the opportunity to make a quiet phone call.

'Is that so!' Jim nodded with interest. His small, piggy eyes registered an opportunity to be grasped.

'Jim!'

'I'll need to go. Thanks for that. It could be a useful bit of information there. I'll give you a call back soon.'

Jim sighed as he looked upstairs in response to Sorcha's call.

'Just for a bit longer,' he mumbled to himself as he trudged up the stairs.

Chapter Ten

Unpleasant News

The following morning was frosty but still. Rosie was glad to see the back of the fierce wind that had been buffeting Erin's Glen for a few days. Her usual cheer returned as she drove to work in her little Mini. Erin's Glen was a grand place to live, she thought contentedly as the town folk waved to her as she passed. It was the convention in the town and surrounding countryside that people waved at passing cars whether they knew the occupants or not. Rosie knew most of the people anyway, and this familiar ritual gave her comfort and a sense of belonging. Her pensive mood from the night before had eased, and Rosie felt buoyed and ready for the day ahead.

After parking outside the presbytery where Father Gerard lived, Rosie hurried into the parish office, which was situated next door between the house and the church. She saw the priest sitting at the large desk by the office window. As she entered, he turned on the office chair to face her. She was about to exclaim a bright 'Good morning' to Father Gerard, but the words died on her lips when she saw the look on his face. His skin was ashen, and he appeared oblivious to her arrival.

He appeared more frail than usual in the oversized leather chair with its high back. After a moment, he looked up from the letter he held.

'What on earth is it, Father?' Rosie's eyes loomed large and full of concern behind her thick glasses as she looked at him intently.

Father Gerard glanced back at her briefly and shook his head slowly, apparently puzzled and shocked by the letter's contents.

'I… I don't know,' he managed to stutter, visibly shaken by what he was reading. Father Gerard usually spoke in a soft, low voice, but it was barely audible today.

Rosie tried to be patient but could no longer resist it and asked, 'May I take a look, Father?' She felt like snatching it from his hands, but her inherent politeness restrained her. Painfully, slowly, he passed the letter to her.

Her first impression of the missive was that it looked incredibly ugly. It was not a handwritten or typed letter, but the words had been made up from chopped-up pieces from a newspaper. They were assorted in size and font and looked oddly random and ill-assorted. Some characters were misplaced capitals, and some were lowercase. Although the words were assembled in this hotch-potch manner, they did spell out a coherent sentence – just a single sentence with an undercurrent of threat that had rattled the priest.

Rosie looked perplexed at the words in front of her, unable to make sense of the brief message.

She read it out slowly:

'I know about you and your secret.'

Father Gerard looked back at her. His head to one side, a look of hurt bewilderment on his face.

'What are they getting at?' Rosie asked him.

Father Gerard appeared to look off into the far distance and shook his head slowly.

'Thirty-five years I've served this parish faithfully. It's as if that counts for nothing.'

Father Gerard sighed deeply as he accepted the letter from Rosie and slowly folded it up. He was seemingly ignoring her question.

Rosie maintained her steady gaze as she observed him tuck the letter into his pocket. She felt a swell of anger and resentment bubble up in defence of this man she had great affection and respect for.

'What are you going to do?' Rosie asked, perhaps a bit more sharply than she intended.

'Pray.' Father Gerard got up from his chair slowly. He appeared suddenly over-burdened and looked older than his sixty years of age. Rosie watched as he left the room, his feet slightly shuffling across the wooden floor.

After the priest had left the room, Rosie stood by the window and followed the sad figure with her gaze as he made his way to the church. Rosie sat down heavily in the chair he had just been occupying.

'Well,' she said to herself. 'I'll be doing more than praying.'

Her previous buoyant mood evaporated. The letter was imprinted on her photographic memory with its butchered graphics and disturbing message. The cold chill of the last evening crept back into her consciousness.

Growing up and living all of her life in a small community had made her sensitive to the nuances of events in the locality and amongst her friends and acquaintances. This letter Father Gerard had received today was deeply troubling. Rosie turned over some of the other concerns in her mind. Mairead McGrath's recent misanthropic behaviour was also a factor. Why was she avoiding going out outside of work hours or socialising? Perhaps caring for her mother was taking its toll. Rosie could identify with the stress of caring for an elderly relative at home. When her mother was alive, Rosie felt she couldn't go out much after work as she needed to provide company for her ailing mother. The guilt she had felt doing something for herself had cancelled out any joy the social event had provided. Rosie sighed in sympathy with Mairead McGrath.

Rosie's thoughts then turned to old Will. The shadow of Will's mysterious departure, absence and presumed death loomed like a background shadow in Rosie's consciousness; it bothered her that no one knew what happened to him. His shop being taken over by a new proprietor had highlighted his disappearance and created a sense of finality that disturbed Rosie. Of course, there was also the ongoing worry about Deirdre. She was a bit of a waif, and it was a shame she had taken up with that lad Sean. Of course, there was nothing Rosie could do about that, and with this realisation, she sighed deeply and looked around her. As Rosie sat at the desk, something caught the corner of her eye. She was aware of a red flashing light as she gazed out the window, mulling over recent events.

'Oh, for goodness' sake, you don't help either!' Rosie was addressing the inanimate and unresponsive answering machine that continued to baffle her. She disliked its random beeps and high-pitched squeaks. The purposes of its many buttons and lights were a mystery to her. She threw her scarf over it and got on with the less technical aspects of her job, like opening letters and writing cheques.

Being a practical woman, Rosie tried to get on with her morning routine tasks. But even so, at regular intervals during the morning, she mused on how to help Father Gerard get to the source of this malicious correspondence. As she typed and filled in forms and arranged for the payment of parish bills, the worry of that letter niggled away at her.

By lunchtime, she decided to do what she usually did in these situations. Get onto her longtime friend, Mary Jo.

Chapter Eleven

Family Arguments

Sorcha sat by the window looking down into the high street. She did this most days. Often, she would sit brushing her long hair with the heavy Victorian hairbrush inherited from her grandmother. It had dense, thick bristles and a beautiful green lacquered back. The slow strokes of the brush through her hair soothed her and sometimes lulled her into a trance. She lost track of time easily. The clock lost all meaning for Sorcha. Instead, her days were measured by sounds and light, and her day usually started with the early morning sounds of the milk being delivered. She liked to hear the milkman whistle and the bottles clink and rattle on the little electric truck – the milk float. It's a funny name for a little truck. Floating milk. How funny, she thought. Just like her thoughts, all floaty. Sorcha continued to brush her hair, but her arm was getting tired. She sat for a few moments with the heavy brush in her hand.

Just as Sorcha's thoughts floated off, she heard a commotion in the street. She pulled herself up and peered out, craning her neck to see who was making all the noise on the pavement below.

Her Jim and Sean were arguing. Their voices bounced off the walls of the quiet shops and houses, still shuttered up from the night before. Sorcha couldn't make out all the words, but she knew it had something to do with Will – her husband's uncle. She remembered Sean was her cousin by marriage, but her head got fuzzy and hurt when she tried to think it all through and what their argument might mean. She didn't often see Sean these days. He didn't come into The Thatch, but she had seen him zigzag down the road late at night on the way back from Shenanigans, the drinking den up the road.

Sorcha refocused on the scene in the street below. She saw Sean push Jim on the shoulder. Jim stepped back. He looked like he was trying to calm Sean down, but Sean hissed something in Jim's face and turned away. He was marching off up the street.

Sorcha tried to think what this might mean but got distracted by the sun. She saw so little sun, especially at this time of year. The sun tracked the day's progress as its light travelled up one wall and down the opposite. Then the night would creep in, but it was all right because she would hear all the cheery voices in the bar downstairs at night. Loneliness was not a problem for her as she had all the familiar noises and voices to listen to, and all she had to do was look out the window to see people she knew. However, that new woman was across the road in Will's shop. Who was she?

Sorcha used to enjoy working behind the bar when she was younger. But her days of pulling pints and chatting to the locals were long gone. Jim didn't pressure her to work. He was so good. He brought her meals and tea and would help her with her bath and hair washing. He understood her. After all the disappointments of the past, she just got incredibly sad. She was so sorry she couldn't talk to people or go out anymore, but Jim just let her be. He didn't fuss with her or force her. Sorcha was grateful for what she saw as his gentle understanding.

As if on cue, Jim bustled in with tea and toast on a tray.

'Here you are, my lovely.'

Sorcha looked at him with gratitude. She meant to ask him something but couldn't remember what. Something important niggled in the back of her brain.

'What is it?' Jim looked at her, breathing heavily from exerting himself, climbing the stairs.

Sorcha just shook her head sadly. Whatever it was she was going to ask him had gone.

'Ah, it'll come to me later, Jim. You know how it is.'

'Right so.' Jim nodded briskly, and just as he was about to go out the door, Sorcha called after him.

'Jim, where did your Uncle Will go?'

Jim looked taken aback. 'Sure, why are you thinking about him, love? He disappeared years ago, leaving that young Sean on his own.'

'Did he die?' Sorcha asked, suddenly concerned and desperate to make sense of the snatches of information swirling about in her head.

'He might as well have. You don't be bothering yourself about all the family stuff from the past. Now, have you got enough toast there? Drink up that tea before it gets cold. I'd best be getting on.'

With that, Jim stepped out of the room and closed the door firmly behind him.

The morning's events had disturbed him, and Sorcha's ramblings weren't helping either.

Sorcha ate her toast slowly and thoughtfully. When she looked out the window again, it returned to her what she had wanted to ask Jim.

'Why *was* he arguing with Sean?'

Chapter Twelve

The Craft of Conversation

Rosie had tried to ring Mary Jo that day but failed to succeed. Mary Jo had a full timetable when she was teaching in school and was in lessons each time Rosie rang the school office. Rosie considered whether she should discuss the priest's business with Mary Jo, but Rosie knew that the nun would respect information shared in confidence. Despite her effusive personality, she was not a 'gab'. A 'gab' was Rosie's word for indiscreet gossip, of which she could safely say neither she nor Mary Jo was. They enjoyed conversations with human interest, but they were not gossiping. Thus, reassured by this train of thought, Rosie was desperate to have a quiet word with her friend.

However, it was not to be. Rosie was due to attend the craft evening at the bookshop. She hadn't had a minute to herself this week. She had intended to pop in to introduce herself to the new owner, but the time had just flown by. Anyway, she'd get to meet her this evening.

It was a quick turnaround after work. Ziggy got a super-fast trot around the park at the end of her road. He was keen to turn back anyway and return home to get his dinner and snooze by the range in the kitchen. Rosie wolfed down her own dinner, a thick soup she had left in the slow cooker while she was out at work. Thus, fortified by a hearty meal, she packed up her quilting bag under the watchful gaze of an ever-hopeful Ziggy. Rosie stopped short and looked back at him, half-open craft bag in hand.

'Not this evening, young man. You are staying here.'

Seeming to understand her every word, Ziggy sloped off to his basket. Curled up with his chin on his front paws, his eyes followed Rosie, his eyebrows wiggling as she darted about the kitchen, picking up items she might need for her evening out.

Before making her way to the front door, she tapped the 'on' switch on the radio and left Ziggy to enjoy a bit of jazz.

Rosie's feet crunched along the icy gravel as she made her way to her Mini, threw her bags onto the passenger seat and set off on the short drive to the shop in town.

The cold had intensified, and Rosie's hands felt frozen as she held onto the strap of her bag and walked across the pavement to the shop. Despite the inclement temperature, Rosie paused outside the shop. She was charmed by the twinkling lights and attractive book display in the window. There was a ring of condensation around the edges of the window, which just blurred and softened the glittering lights to a warm, soft glow.

'You've put old Will to shame, love. What a pretty display!'

With this warm and genuine compliment, Rosie greeted Marie for the first time as the younger woman opened the door for her visitor.

Taking in her thick velvet dress and heavy boots, Rosie's gaze settled momentarily on the silver pendant around her neck. Rosie had seen one like that before. It would come to her later; her photographic memory never let her down.

With her usual self-effacing manner, Marie murmured her thanks and turned to the members of the group already assembled. Rosie could see Deirdre, sitting still in her coat, looking slightly uncomfortable, Kay Byrne, the music and dance teacher from the school, and as she was taking this in, Mary Jo bounded towards her, arms open for a hug.

'Great to see you, Rosie. All the girls are here. Kay could make it, too, so the more, the merrier! Take a seat.' Rosie was used to Mary Jo taking the lead in social situations, and Marie didn't seem put out.

Marie had prepared a big pot of steaming tea for them all, and Deirdre had brought a tin of homemade traybake cakes. After some fussing regarding enquiries about the preferred strength of tea, quantities of milk and sugar required and plates passed around, the group settled quietly to munch through the cakes and mumble their thanks through mouthfuls of rich fruit and moist, dark sponge.

Thinking she really should be a more assertive host, Marie thanked everyone for attending, especially on such a cold night. Marie didn't need to worry about saying too much as the conversation flowed easily, facilitated by Mary Jo's wish to bring everyone together to enjoy each other's company and hone their skills.

'Deirdre, tell us about these delicious cakes. What's in them, and what are they called?' Mary Jo fixed her warm gaze on Deirdre, her cake held aloft as she asked the question.

Deirdre explained that it was her own recipe; the cakes were made with oats, flour, dried fruit, and sweet spices such as nutmeg and cinnamon.

'But they are so moist!' Rosie remarked. 'How do you manage that then?'

Deirdre smiled shyly. 'Ah well, that's my magic secret.'

The ladies were intrigued and sat waiting for Deirdre to divulge.

Deirdre continued, 'Well, the secret is in the name, 'Porridge Cakes'. I make up the oats as a porridge, add the other ingredients and bake them. That's what makes them so squishy and moist. It's a great way to use up leftover porridge.'

'And you made that up yourself?' Kay Byrne clarified.

'Oh aye, it was a bit of an experiment, but it seems to have worked.' Deirdre blushed slightly, a little embarrassed by all the attention.

'You've got talent there, girl,' Mary Jo confirmed, and the group of happy women sat for a few seconds quietly enjoying the delights of the succulent, fruity cakes, all munching happily.

Marie looked around her contentedly, happy to have some human company and, in her quiet way, eager to learn more about this community she had moved into.

There was some general chit-chat about the St Patrick's Day Parade and the required preparations. Kay Byrne was keen to embroider motifs for the dresses to be worn by her girls doing the Irish dancing display. Most parents made arrangements for their daughters privately, but it was a costly business. The dancing pumps and intricately embroidered dresses were a pretty penny, and Kay tried to help the less affluent families by embroidering the motifs for them. Besides, she enjoyed it.

The vigilant Mary Jo noticed Kay's generosity, 'You're very good doing that for the girls.' Mary Jo nodded at the stitching held in Kay's hands, the jewel-like colours of the threads glinting in the lights.

In response to Mary Jo's admiration of her skill and philanthropic nature, the dance and music teacher was dismissive. 'Sure, I'm trying to stop smoking, and this gives me something to take my mind off lighting up.'

Mary Jo had never been afflicted with a nicotine addiction, so the conversation moved on to the shop and Marie.

'What brought you to Erin's Glen?' the nun enquired as she looked kindly at the newcomer.

Despite Mary Jo's warm smile and kind, bright eyes. Marie seemed shy and tongue-tied, not quite sure how to respond.

The group waited, needles poised, faces expectant as Marie thrashed about trying to articulate an answer. In truth, they were all rather intrigued by this lady from London. She sounded very posh and had such refined ideas that they were keen to get to know her better. The best Marie could do was mumble something about making a fresh start, having a new challenge, and it being time to 'move on'.

None the wiser, deciding it was best not to pry the kind group of ladies carried on with their stitching.

After a moment of quiet, the sound of a ticking clock, the clicking of Marie's knitting needles and the gentle creaking of a shop sign outside being the only noise, Mary Jo piped up, 'Speaking of visitors, I talked to Mrs Kirkpatrick at the post office, and she had been chatting with Mrs Blaney, who runs the B&B; Mrs Blaney has a visitor from Spain. Isabella Santos, that's a lovely name, isn't it?'

Rosie was about to ask questions when the sound of mewing piqued her interest. Marie, relieved to have something take her out of the limelight, stood up, intending to fetch the little cat who seemed to have adopted her. 'I've had a visitor myself!' Marie smiled at the circle of friendly faces. 'Let me show you.'

Marie left the group and climbed the stairs, searching for the fur ball. She glanced around the small flat, but he proved elusive. Marie caught a glimpse of the end of his tail as he disappeared under the low double bed in Marie's bedroom with a cat's typical perverseness.

She returned to the group, but their attention had moved away from the furry enigma. Prompted by the scene in the street, they had abandoned their craft projects. Now, they stood by the window, mesmerised by softly falling snow. The female group formed a magical little tableau illuminated by the soft fairy lights in the window.

After a few seconds of admiring the freshly fallen snow, the practical streak of the Irish countrywomen kicked in, and they shook off the spell of the moment, suddenly concerned about the snow and the difficulties this would present getting back to their respective homes.

'Right, girls, there's room for the three of you in the Mini. I'll get you back safe and sound.' Rosie packed her bag, thanked Marie, and ushered her friends back into the night. She was mentally working out her route to each of their houses. She was concerned about getting them all home safely and was determined to get Mary Jo on her own and have a quiet word.

Father Gerard's letter was still on her mind, and she was keen to get Mary Jo's perspective on the whole sorry business.

So, with cheerful goodbyes and warm expressions of gratitude to their host, the four women piled into the little car. The three passengers sat under bundles of craft bags, muffled in thick coats, scarves, and hats. Their breaths steaming in the cold air. The radio blared out as Rosie turned the ignition on, and the car spluttered and juddered into life.

'Sorry, girls,' Rosie shouted above the catchy céilí music. 'It always does that; it shocks me every time!' They all laughed, well used to Rosie's lack of technical expertise, and Mary Jo leaned over to lower the volume.

The ladies chatted happily as the Mini travelled around a white and glistening Erin's Glen, depositing each one safely home for the night.

CHAPTER THIRTEEN

Late-Night Reflections

The chatter of the little group faded into the distance, and Marie watched as the four women bundled themselves into the small car. After a couple of false starts, its throaty engine spluttered off up the road, and Marie was left standing by the window of her shop looking out onto an empty street. The snow was falling fast now, and the silence and gentle beauty of the scene spellbound her.

Marie jumped as she felt a warm tickle of fur around her ankles. 'There you are! You are a proving to be a will-o'-the-wisp, aren't you?' Marie bent down and stroked the cat's warm back. 'That's what I'll call you – Willow. That is unless anyone comes to claim you. What do you think?' Willow sat down to consider this proposition and purred as if in agreement.

Marie busied herself, clearing away the cups and plates, washing them up, and stacking them neatly on the draining board in the small kitchen just off the shop. Her hands were completing the chores routinely as she mentally reviewed the events and conversation of the evening. She concluded that despite the sudden finish due to the snow, it had been a success. She did worry that perhaps her inability to tell them more about herself would create some mistrust or resentment, but the women were friendly and easy to get along with. Marie's reticence and hesitancy had not seemed to put them off. In truth, Marie had basked in the warmth of their chatter and banter. The gentle rhythm of her days and the quiet evenings in Erin's Glen were working a subdued but powerful healing magic on Marie. She felt that, in time, she would get braver and be able to open up a little more. The anxiety and stress she had felt so often during her days in London were subsiding, replaced by feelings of contentment.

After the tidy-up, Marie ascended the short flight of winding wooden stairs to her little flat above the shop. The warmth of her log burner hit her as she approached the level of her bijou lounge. Even after just a few weeks, it felt like home. She cast an appreciative look around her living space. The flat was up in the eaves of the building, and the low, sloping ceiling created a cosy area to retreat to in the evenings. An overstuffed two-seater sofa and matching armchair provided ample space for her to sit, read, knit, or listen to the radio. A warm hand-knitted shawl was draped over the back of the chair, adding colour and texture to the simple furnishings. A round dining table was in another corner by a large dormer window.

After a moment spent admiring her little nest, Marie padded through a low archway to the kitchen. Willow was treated to a saucer of milk, and Marie boiled up the kettle and made herself a cup of chamomile tea. Marie spent a few moments stirring some golden honey into the hot, amber liquid, enjoying the richness of the colour and the soothing aroma as she moved the spoon slowly around the mug. She took her cup of tea and sat by the window in her lounge, gazing out onto Slieve Cairn, the now snowy mountain visible as a hazy outline illuminated by its dusting of snow. Marie had a good view of the mountain from the back windows of the building and enjoyed contemplating its contours at different times of the day and into the night.

She settled into a trancelike state as she focused on the scene outside her window. Like a child charmed by the falling flakes in a snow globe, Marie was entranced by the feather-like wisps of white drifting down in the darkness, illuminated by the bright moon. As she sat with Willow curled up on her lap, Marie's mind drifted back to the months and weeks before she left England. It had been an eventful lead-up to her solo journey to this little valley she was now thinking of as home.

'How *did* it all start?' she asked herself. Her reflections were prompted by the questions she was batting off this evening. 'Why *was* she here, and what did she hope to accomplish?'

It all started with her mum getting ill a couple of years ago. Her father had passed away some years before that. Her mum, Nancy, was now in her late seventies and had never recovered from the grief of losing her husband of nearly fifty years. Nancy's behaviour became increasingly bizarre, and her memory deteriorated so severely that she forgot to eat or wash. She was diagnosed with Alzheimer's, and a brisk social worker found Nancy a place in a nursing home where she could be cared for. Marie had struggled with guilt about her mother's move into the home, and it was after her mother was taken into the nursing home that Marie had the biggest shock of her life.

The hissing and crackle of the fire, the warmth, and the soft purring of the furry bundle in her lap lulled Marie into a sleepy, trancelike state. Thoughts that had previously caused her heart to flutter into pounding palpitations now became a more comfortable part of her story. A series of events, choices, and decisions led her to this small town in the valley. Although much of it had been difficult, she was grateful they had led her to this charming and comfortable place she was now thinking of as home. She began to feel more at ease with the train of happenings and sighed as she contemplated the momentous revelations of recent years.

'Ow!' Marie screeched suddenly, shocked by the mercurial Willow, who had unawares caught her with his claws as he jumped off her lap. He now stood in the middle of the living room, back arched and hackles raised.

Just then, the gentle chimes of the clock tower slowly and methodically struck eleven. As the rhythmic chimes sounded out, Marie picked Willow up and soothed him, stroking him softly.

'Oh, you silly puss, calm down,' Marie chided gently.

When his meows and hisses subsided, the night returned to the complete quiet Marie had been enjoying just a few moments before, but the spell was broken.

'Come on. Time for bed.' And with that, Marie closed the small glass door of the wood burner and headed off to her bedroom with Willow at her heels.

Chapter Fourteen

A Chilling Discovery

Dan had passed the magical snowy night in the less-than-magical interior of the local police station. He had sat typing up reports dutifully. The dull pace of nights at the small-town station suited him perfectly fine. He was never a whizz on the keyboard, and the lack of pressure a long twelve-hour shift provided meant he made fewer mistakes due to rushing. That being said, the Tipp-Ex correction fluid was close to hand at the ready when he bashed down on the wrong key. However, tonight, he was in the flow, and the tapping of the keys punctuated by the roll and ding of the typewriter was the only sound that broke into the quiet of the night as he worked through his reports.

Now and then, he would get up and stride about the bare room painted in a sickly shade of green. Occasionally, he would do a few quick press-ups on the floor. All in an effort to stay awake and keep fit as best he could.

At 7 am sharp, Seargent McKenna arrived to relieve the constable of his duties and get a handover of the events of the night before.

'Nothing much to report, sir.' Dan recounted some calls concerning break-downs on the road due to the bad weather, but they had all been sorted with a few phone calls and the drivers involved had headed home safely.

Both men concluded it had been a quiet night due to the bad weather keeping everyone indoors.

Dan duly got his bike out, pulled on his coat, hat and gloves and set off home, looking forward to a hot cup of tea and a fry-up as was his routine.

Dan was making the familiar cycle home along the high street and was approaching The Thatch when an unfamiliar snow-covered mound on the white footpath caught his attention.

'That'll be that Jim Noonan leaving rubbish out the front.' Dan tutted to himself but came to a halt to look more closely. Something about the shape alerted him that it could be something more sinister.

Meanwhile, that same morning, Rosie was getting ready to leave home to walk Ziggy. As usual, Rosie had her day mapped out. She would give Ziggy a good walk and then get off to work. She wanted to stop at Marie's shop on the way to work that morning to thank her for the evening before. Rosie was not fazed by a bit of snow or ice. The journey to the parish office was short; she would go on foot to avoid mishaps in the Mini.

'And you, you little tinker, get to come to work with Mammy today.' Ziggy responded with a wag of his tail, his amber eyes glinting back at Rosie in appreciation. Father Gerard loved seeing Ziggy; the fluffy canine was no trouble in the office, usually happy to snooze under the desk at Rosie's feet. If she walked to work, she might as well take Ziggy along. This would save her from taking him out far later on what would probably be another cold night.

As Rosie pulled on her snow boots and attached Ziggy's lead, the sense of foreboding returned. She couldn't shake off her concern about the malicious message the priest had received the day before.

She was utterly perplexed. 'Why?' She kept turning the question over in her mind. Why and who? Who would feel motivated to send such an unsettling message to such a kind and genuine man?

Ziggy was keen to get out, but he protested against being squeezed into the indignity of his tartan coat. Already warm in her Aran wool sweater, thick checkered coat, scarf and hat, Rosie was flushed with the heated effort of grabbling with unwilling doggy limbs to get him into the restrictive coat he hated.

'You need to go on a diet, you little piggy,' Rosie chided affectionately. Ziggy wasn't too concerned. They knew no human could resist Ziggy's charms regarding cadging treats and tasty leftovers. His soulful, honeyed eyes could soften the hardest of hearts.

'I feel like I've done a day's work already, you rapscallion.' Rosie puffed breathlessly as she paused by her front door.

Once she had gotten her breath back, tidied her hair in the hall mirror, and locked her front door, they were off. They descended the hill down from her bungalow. It was still quite dark on the cold January morning, but the snow gave the scene an eerie glow. Rosie strode along confidently, and within a few minutes, the string of lights that illuminated Rainbow Row were in sight. The sight of the cheerfully painted shopfronts, the windows reflecting the lights, made Rosie's heart swell with pride for the little town she had spent her life in. Rosie stopped momentarily as Ziggy investigated a particularly interesting lamp post, and she paused to admire the familiar sight embellished by nature; the higgledy-piggledy line of buildings was snuggled under a thick blanket of snow this morning. Although Christmas was now just a memory, the scene before her would have made a delightful yuletide picture. Rosie sighed and smiled. Erin's Glen was a grand place to live. After a few moments of musing on the charms of Erin's Glen's main street, Rosie and Ziggy continued on their way towards the town.

A streak of grey light swept across the sky as they turned the corner onto the high street. Rosie squinted through her thick glasses and could make out the outline of Dan, the policeman, walking towards a mound in the snow outside The Thatch. Immediately, her heart lurched, alarmed by the unfamiliar sight and an intuitive sense that something was very wrong. She quickened her step, Ziggy in tow. With a dog's opportunistic awareness of an owner's distraction, Ziggy pulled hard on the lead and unbalanced his owner. Rosie slipped in the icy snow as Ziggy darted off, quick as a flash, straight down the street to investigate.

At that exact moment, the full significance of what Dan had seen lying on the pavement had become revealed to him. 'Ah Lord, please no!' he murmured to himself as he approached the unidentified shape in the snow. Before going a step further, he glanced around. No footprints other than his own were visible. The steady, heavy snowfall during the night had obliterated any footprints. He then moved towards the focus of his attention. Meanwhile, Rosie lay for a few seconds winded on her back, unable to greet Dan or call Ziggy back.

Dan stepped back to scan the shape he was looking at and was startled by a high-pitched squeak. He saw a dark furry blur dart away from under his feet – Ziggy! The nosey canine gave a quick sniff. Scurrying around the prostrate form, tail wagging and nose twitching.

When Rosie regained her breath, she was mortified by her dog's unruly behaviour. As she stood up and hurried closer to Dan and Ziggy, she was horrified by what she saw. Her brisk walk had warmed Rosie, but in that split second, she was chilled to the bone, and the cause was not just the icy weather. 'I'm so sorry, Dan; he pulled the lead out of my hand and took me by surprise.' Despite her urge to lasso her naughty dog, Rosie couldn't resist looking at what Dan had just revealed. She recognised the jacket and hair but said nothing. Her shrewd eyes swept over the entire scene, imprinting it onto her memory. Pausing, she quickly made the sign of the cross. Ziggy continued to fuss around the form lying on the ground. Knowing he was in trouble, he glanced at his owner and ran up the street. Rosie, huffing and puffing up the path in hot pursuit, lifted her hand by way of farewell to Dan and continued up the footpath, shouting after Ziggy.

When Dan recovered from this unexpected interruption, he sprang back into life; the policeman got in close and crouched down to get a better view and investigate further. He brushed a layer of snow away and revealed more of the jacket's black leather. The leather was stained with blood that had frozen fast to the material that Dan recognised as a jacket worn by Sean. He continued to lightly flick away more snow, moving along to confirm what he already knew: the back of Sean's dark-haired head. The hair was matted with blood and flecked with ice and snow.

The street was still quiet, with just a few signs of early morning life stirring in the distance. As Dan crouched by the lifeless form, fresh snow began to fall lightly, already sprinkling the exposed wound with a light dusting of snow. Although Dan had a low opinion of the young man who lay by his feet, he felt a stab of sadness and a deep sense of loss at the end of life so prematurely and violently.

Dan didn't need to touch the body more than he already had. He would leave further investigation to the specialist officers and the pathologist, who would arrive promptly. No doubt, this would be one for a post-mortem and the coroner. It crossed Dan's mind that Sean could have fallen, the worse for wear with a drink on an icy night. The blow to his head could have been made on impact with the pavement.

Perhaps Sean lay there winded, with just enough strength to turn over. If he was concussed on a freezing cold night, he might have died of hyperthermia in an intoxicated state.

Possibly. But considering Sean's lifestyle and his secrets, it was more likely to be foul play. Dan quickly dismissed these premature conclusions and focused on the task at hand. His job now was to secure the scene, inform his superior officer back at the station and ask some questions immediately.

Satisfied that he had made the necessary preliminary observations, Dan moved to the wide double doors of The Thatch and hollered inside the entranceway for Jim. He heard a female voice swear gently from upstairs, obviously disturbed by the volume and urgency of his voice at such an early hour. Katie, the barmaid, shuffled down in her slippers, startled to see the policeman's sturdy form fill up the entranceway. As she looked at him, her anger turned to shock and concern.

'I need to use the phone.' Dan pushed past her. Usually the epitome of civility, Katie was further taken aback by Dan's uncharacteristic brusqueness.

Dan rang the station and informed his superior of the serious matter.

Dan realised, without being told, that his shift was now extended. He would have a full day ahead of him, supporting his chief. As one of the few full-time officers in a small country town, Dan understood that the burden of the investigation would fall on him. His colleagues in the cities and larger towns had bigger fish to fry. He reminded himself that this could have been accidental, but he was not convinced. And so, he was already in full-on questioning mode.

His first job was to secure the scene. The police photographer would arrive soon, followed by the pathologist and staff to remove the remains to the police morgue. He asked Katie to fetch a clean plastic sack, and he went out and threw that over the body. After that, he made a quick phone call home to let his wife know he would be delayed. Dan returned to Katie, who stood frozen by the pub doorway.

'Step in a second. I need to ask you a few questions.'

Katie gulped as the seasoned guard focused on her, notebook and pencil in hand.

Dan took a deep breath. It was going to be a long day ahead.

Chapter Fifteen

Shock Waves

There were virtually no cars along the high street on this snowy morning. The unusual lack of traffic created an eerie quiet. The thick carpet of snow muffled any sounds there were. The combined effect resulted in a hushed and watchful atmosphere. Once Rosie had caught up with her naughty dog, she doubled back down along Rainbow Row and stepped out into the road, circling past Sean's body, now covered in plastic. All Rosie could hear was Dan's low, throaty voice as he asked Katie some questions.

Rosie glanced over the road and saw Marie's outline standing by the shop window, looking out into the street. Rosie hesitated momentarily and then decided to go over to break the news in person. Rosie felt for the new woman in town and thought it best to tell her in person about this distressing discovery opposite her shop. Seeing Rosie approach, Marie unbolted her shop door and opened it with a concerned look. The jolly bell tinkled as usual and seemed at odds with the sombreness of the scene out in the street.

'Are you all right, love?' Rosie's concerned face looked into Marie's eyes.

Marie quickly nodded and asked, 'What's going on?'

Rosie thought it best to get straight to the point. 'It's Sean. Deirdre's boyfriend. He's been found dead in the street.' With this, Marie convulsed into tears. Rosie guided Marie to one of the armchairs Marie had provided for customers wishing to peruse books comfortably. Ever the practical helper, Rosie sprang into action; tissues were proffered, and a glass of water fetched from Marie's kitchenette behind the shop counter.

'Oh, dear, there you are. You've had such a shock, and you only just arrived in the place,' Rosie soothed and tutted, stroking the other woman's hair with motherly concern.

Marie, usually composed and reserved, only cried harder. Somehow, Rosie's display of support and the maternal quality of her presence opened a floodgate. The tears flowed, and Marie gulped and gasped for breath, overwhelmed by the depth of her feeling. All the emotions Marie had kept tightly locked up over the past few years seemed to flow out in copious tears and sobs.

Rosie waited, a comforting presence by Marie's side as she expelled the pent-up feelings. Rosie realised she knew very little about this enigma from London. She resolved to find out more and provide companionship to this seemingly lonely and unconnected woman. Rosie read the newspapers and watched the news. Terrible things happened in the big city Marie hailed from, and this small-town event, no matter how distressing, could not have been the worst Marie was ever exposed to.

As Rosie considered her observations silently, Marie regained her composure with deep breaths, sighs, and sniffles. The sobs subsided into whimpers. At last, the vast tide of emotion had passed over her, and she looked spent and exhausted.

In the style typical of Marie, she immediately apologised to Rosie for her display of emotion and attempted to get up quickly and step back into her shop owner role.

Rosie gently pushed her down into the comfortable but shabby old leather chair.

'Now, never you mind about that. You've had a shock. These things can set us off on a track that can lead back to old hurts, maybe?' Rosie paused. Marie responded with a nod of agreement, and Rosie's assumptions were confirmed. This young woman has a sad past.

'You let the tears out, and I'm sure you'll feel better.' With these words of comfort, Rosie set about making some tea and chatting about the weather – a comfortingly neutral topic to ease the intensity of this emotional morning. Rosie's questions could wait until later.

'I don't want to delay you, Rosie. Are you working today?' Marie looked confused.

'Don't you be worrying. I've got plenty of time, and I wanted to make sure you didn't get too much of a shock,' Rosie handed Marie a mug of tea.

Marie sipped the comforting brew and looked tearfully at Rosie, 'What do you think happened to him?'

Rosie shook her head slowly and thoughtfully, 'At this stage, only the good Lord knows. He's, err, I mean, he *was* a heavy drinker. He might well have fallen over drunk and died of the cold. He wouldn't be the first.' Rosie shuddered at the thought of the young man dying alone in the street without a soul near him.

Ziggy had been watching the scene with a gentle canine interest. He had been looking soulfully at Marie with his amber eyes, and now that Marie had calmed down, he felt brave enough to approach her with licks and nuzzles. Marie appreciated his furry concern and rewarded him now with her full attention. 'Well, you're a cutey.' Marie smiled. She loved dogs and was charmed by his glossy fur, sparkling eyes, and reassuring presence. Ziggy was relishing the attention, tickles, and fuss. His eyes slid in the direction of some treats nearby.

'Don't be feeding him!' Rosie noted the doggy biscuits on the counter. The shop was dog-friendly. Marie was a shrewd shop owner who knew that opening her doors to dog owners would only increase her shop's footfall and potential spending.

'It took me ages to get him into his coat today – what a carry-on!' Ziggy looked back resentfully at his owner. His tail no longer wagging, eyes fixed imploringly on the jar of biscuits, so near yet so far. His crestfallen face seemed to say 'Spoilsport.' Rosie just tutted and smiled indulgently as she grabbed his lead and wound it around her hand.

'I'll get off now, love, if you're feeling a bit better?' In truth, Rosie was taken aback by Marie's powerfully emotional response to the news and worried about this mysterious lady she hardly knew.

'Yes, I'm sorry for getting so wrought up about someone I don't know. Silly of me.' Marie shook her head as she apologised.

'Never you worry about that, love. It shows you have a heart.' And with those words of comfort, Rosie made her way to the door.

With order duly resumed in the bookshop, Rosie felt she could carry on to the parish office. She had promised Marie she would pop in on the way home. With these assurances made, and after a warm hug at the door, Rosie was off.

Marie stood by the door. Blue lights were flashing across the street, and some locals huddled in small groups along the street were discussing the chilling discovery made that morning.

Chapter Sixteen

Sharing Thoughts

Despite the weather, The Carmelite Convent of Our Lady of the Immaculate Conception Girls' School was functioning as usual. In the early hours, local farmers had cleared the worst of the snow away with their tractors and heavy vehicles. Sturdy four-by-fours and Land Rovers had gotten the girls to school, and families doubled up school runs as needed. A chain of phone calls around the small community ensured no one was left stranded at home. 'Snow days' were not a tradition in Erin's Glen, much to staff and students' disappointment.

So, the familiar routine of morning assembly, prayers and lessons carried on. The details of the dramatic events of that morning were, as yet, unknown to most of the school community. Most people avoided driving through the high street on the way to school and took another route as a matter of course. Dan resolved to be discreet. He hesitated about visiting Deirdre at work to inform her of his grisly find that morning, but he felt he needed to see her in person – and quickly.

He did not want some eejit blurting out the news to her before he could speak with her properly. So, he cycled the short distance to the school. He could have taken the police car, but arriving on his bike would attract less attention. He turned over in his mind how he would approach her. The school building, a modern flat-roofed affair, was quiet. He parked his bike by the front doors. The snow crunched under his feet as he made his way around to the side of the school building. He tapped on the kitchen door. He could hear chattering voices inside. The glass in the door was steamed up, and the smell of bacon cooking drifted out. It was a comforting aroma that almost took his mind off the news he was about to deliver. But he realised he had lost his appetite today.

Deirdre spotted him first through the kitchen window. She glanced sideways and then approached the door, opening it to a serious-looking Dan. 'I need to speak to you, Deirdre.' The young woman nodded and turned her back, indicating for him to follow her to a quieter spot. Steady and dependable, Dan was an uncle-like figure to the young Deirdre; they usually greeted each other with some gentle banter. But today, he maintained his sombre expression and slow rolling gait as he followed her into the kitchen.

Dan broke the news as she sat at a table in a cubicle at the back of the kitchen, reserved for kitchen staff meals and breaks. Dan was a little taken aback by her expressionless acceptance of the news. She listened to what he had to say and nodded. He put her lack of emotion down to shock. Dan had questions for Deirdre, but he would call by at her home later. The questions could wait until then.

He left Deirdre alone for a moment while he went to speak to the cook, Maggie. Who assured him she would look after Deirdre and get her a lift home. Maggie looked shaken and upset when Dan briefly shared what had happened with her. Dan then excused himself and spoke with the principal, Miss McGrath. He then returned to the kitchen to see how Deirdre was bearing up. He sat with her at the table where he had broken the news about her partner's death. Deirdre sat with him silently, her coat on and bag on her knees, waiting for a lift home.

After being informed of the news, Miss McGrath needed to speak with her vice-principal, Mary Jo. The senior staff member reined in her emotions and got on with the tasks at hand. Her immediate concern was ensuring the girls were safe and maintaining a calm atmosphere in the school. She had clarified with Dan that there was no threat to the students or staff at the school. Miss McGrath moved through the school with her usual tranquil composure. She immediately went to Mary Jo's classroom and asked for her to come to her office. The girls, senses alert to anything unusual, were watchful and curious as Mary Jo excused herself from the classroom and went to the principal's office. The door was closed for quite some time, and when Mary Jo emerged, her usually cheerful expression was sombre and downcast.

She caught sight of Dan making to leave by the side door. At her call, he came over to her. Mary Jo was a trusted friend. He was relieved to see her familiar face and share some of the burdens of his morning. They spoke by the door in hushed whispers. The school entrance lobby was silent. Occasionally, one student or staff member would pass through on the way to do an errand or visit the bathroom. The nun and policeman huddled in a conversation, eliciting some curious stares, but no one interrupted them.

After a few minutes, the old friends drew apart and expressed their mutual thanks and goodbyes.

Mary Jo immediately went to the empty staff room. Lessons were still in progress; this was her only chance to have a private telephone conversation, so she took the opportunity.

Mary Jo only had to wait for one ringtone before she heard the familiar voice answer.

'St Bridget's Parish Office, Rosie speaking. How may I help you?' At this point, Mary Jo usually joked about Rosie's posh 'telephone voice'. But not today.

'Have you heard the news yet, Rosie?'

Rosie gave Mary Jo all the facts of the morning, and Mary Jo filled her in on events at the school.

They both pondered on who would have wanted to do away with Sean.

'Of course, he had many enemies,' Rosie mused expansively.

'Who?' Mary Jo pressed.

'Well, I don't know exactly, but I think he was involved in a lot of shady business.'

'But how do you know that, Rosie? What evidence do you have? We can all make assumptions about people, but we need to be able to substantiate them.'

Rosie went silent for a moment. 'You're right. It's all just conjecture, putting two and two together and getting five. He disappeared off that time a few years ago, and we never knew where he went. Also, there was that fire at the car workshop—'

Mary Jo cut her off by commenting, 'Yes, but that was when Will, his father, was still in charge; you can't blame all that business on Sean.'

Both fell silent as they considered the situation.

Rosie broke the brief silence, 'What about Jim? Has Dan spoken to him yet? Sean and Jim had a big bust-up years ago. Sure, Sean wouldn't darken the door of The Thatch. He used Shenanigans as his drinking den.'

Mary Jo conceded the truth of these observations. She shared that, as far as she knew, Dan had yet to speak with Jim.

'Don't you think that's strange? Sean was found right outside The Thatch? I'm going to find out what Jim was up to last night,' Rosie pondered.

Again, Mary Jo countered the question with her own rhetorical question, 'So you think Jim bashed Sean on the head and left him there right outside his pub? If he did it, he's been a bit sloppy about clearing up after him; God forgive me.'

At this, Mary Jo looked to heaven and made the sign of the cross, sorry to speak disrespectfully about Sean's remains.

Rosie reflected on how badly Sean treated his live-in girlfriend. 'Could you imagine all that anger that must have built up?' Rosie was warming to the drama this conjecture entailed. Her eyes were getting wider behind her thick lenses. 'She might have just snapped and done him in.'

'Possibly. But come on, Rosie, wee Deirdre is not murderer material. I'd be shocked.' The nun tutted, disagreeing with her theatrical friend.

'That new girl from London took the news very badly. She was distraught when I told her who it was that had been found. I wonder what all that was about. She seemed genuine enough, but I do wonder...?' Rosie reflected on Marie's tearful reaction to the news that morning.

'What? Marie? Sure, she's a lovely girl!' Mary Jo was taken aback that Rosie would even suggest that this mild-mannered, book-loving lady could have anything to do with this shady affair.

'Did Marie even know Sean anyway?' the nun questioned.

'Perhaps that's why she's in Erin's Glen?' her friend rejoined. 'And...' Rosie was searching for something concrete to back up her vague suspicions but was drawing a blank. 'We don't know anything about her,' was all she could offer.

Mary Jo's silence was comment enough on her friend's suggestions that Marie was involved in Sean's death.

After a few seconds of pondering, Rosie acceded to her friend, 'No, you're right, Marie Jo.'

Again, Rosie and Mary Jo fell silent. There was a lot to think about. In the meantime, both women agreed that Sean was not well-liked. In truth, it could have been a fight with anyone who happened to be out that snowy night. He hung about with a dodgy crowd at Shenanigans.

Rosie's mind then leapfrogged to their recent conversation about Father Gerard's malicious note as they considered the cause of Sean's death. 'Do you think Sean could have been behind that nasty letter?' she asked.

Quick as a flash, Mary Jo was reminded of the other reason she had phoned Rosie.

Father Gerard was not the only one to receive a poison pen letter. Mary Jo had seen an identical one that morning.

Chapter Seventeen

Questions

Earlier in the morning, before his visit to the school, Dan had been busy securing the crime scene outside The Thatch. Ensuring, as best he could, that the small community was not in danger from some wild man on the rampage was high on his list of priorities, and the policeman carried out his duties conscientiously.

His next task was to speak with the bar proprietor, Jim.

So far, the only representative from The Thatch was Katie, the barmaid. She had stood in the hallway answering Dan's questions.

'Where is Jim Noonan this morning?'

Katie informed Dan that Jim had left late yesterday morning to attend a trade conference in the main town about thirty miles away. He was due to drive home late last night, but he had rang and asked Katie to stay the night at The Thatch to keep an ear out for Sorcha and bring her breakfast in the morning.

'Is that usual?' Jim wanted to know.

Katie assured Dan that this was routine enough for her to leave some personal bits at her place of work in case she was asked to stay over to lock up and keep an eye on Sorcha. A staff room was reserved for this very occurrence.

Dan went on to ask Katie about the details of the evening before. When he questioned her about unusual noises, she shook her head. The barmaid had not seen or heard anything unusual the night before except for the snow. Due to the weather, she had closed up early.

'If anything, it was really quiet last night. Not a peep from anyone after 10 pm,' Katie confirmed and then stood looking at Dan. She appeared to be at a loss for words, which was unusual for her.

Katie stood with her arms folded across her.

'So that's when you locked up then?'

Katie hesitated for a moment. 'Aye.' She nodded, swallowing hard.

'Are you sure you locked up the doors here at 10 pm?' Dan shot the question at her with some urgency, and seeing her face crumple, he softened his tone. 'I know it's a shock, Katie, but we need to know the facts to find who did this.'

Katie took a breath. 'Sorry, yes, it's the shock. I locked up at 10 pm. I'm sure. And I didn't hear a thing. Sorry, Dan.'

Dan took a moment to look at her. Katie stood with downcast eyes; it was hard to read her expression.

'Okay, thanks, Katie. I'll call later if I need to ask more questions.' Dan ambled off with his slow, swaying gait, walking thoughtfully and considering the answers he'd just elicited.

'So, Jim was away. How convenient,' Dan muttered to himself. He made a mental note to get onto the trade fair folks and learn more about Jim Noonan's whereabouts last night.

In the meantime, he made his way along the snowy street down to Shenanigans.

Again, Dan had to thump loudly on the door of this bar to rouse the owner. The policeman waited impatiently, hearing shouts from inside and heavy footsteps approaching the door. At last, the door was cracked open, and two sleepy grey eyes peered through at him. Seeing it was the police, the door opened fully, and the young redheaded owner stepped outside. Dan eyed the young man with some distaste. A heavy parka had been thrown over some blue pyjamas, and the young, ruddy face was creased from lack of sleep, a severe hangover, or both. Dan asked the proprietor where he had been the previous evening without explanation. Dan's questions were primarily met with one-word answers from the laconic owner of Shenanigans, who confirmed that he had been working behind the bar the night before. Dan continued to ask specifically about Sean.

Dan was told that Sean had been drinking in Shenanigans the previous evening and that he had left at about 11 pm. Gerry, the young man in charge of Shenanigans, tapped his foot impatiently and dragged hard on a roll-up, eyes squinting. Whether the sensitivity of his eyes was due to the smoke or the daylight out at the front of the bar. Dan wasn't sure. But it was clear the barman was keen to finish the conversation promptly. Gerry scuttled back into the dark environs of the bar at Dan's bidding, disappearing into the gloom.

Dan followed him in; the smell of stale beer and cigarette smoke hung in the air. He paused and took a cursory glance around. Various rock posters were on the walls, primarily long-haired males in outlandish outfits; as far as Dan was concerned, they all needed a good haircut and a box around the ears. But Dan knew his opinions were old-fashioned and kept them to himself.

Gerry was now busying himself with the washing-up abandoned from the night before. Water gushing into a sink behind the bar. Dan tutted involuntarily and made his way towards the bar, noticing his feet sticking to the carpet as he walked.

Dan tapped the bar thoughtfully and paused as he continued to look around and then watch Gerry. The young man kept his eyes fixed on the washing-up. Eventually, Dan broke the silence and asked Gerry, 'Did Sean have much on the slate here?'

Slowly, Gerry dried his hands and pulled a ledger out from under the till. Running his finger down a list of names, he confirmed that Sean had run up a hefty bill.

'Did that not bother you?' Dan questioned; this time, his eyes were narrowed in suspicion.

Gerry appeared nonchalant. 'No, not really. He told me he was coming into some money. The shop was sold, and old Will is presumed dead, so he'd get the dosh; no worries, man, it was all with the legal bods, but the money was coming his way for sure. It was only a matter of time. Sean was a mate.' Gerry shrugged his shoulders and picked up a towel to dry some glasses.

'Was he now?' Dan nodded slowly, keeping his gaze fixed on the rumpled-looking Gerry.

Behind the closed doors that separated the bar from the living quarters upstairs, a female voice called out, 'Gerry…' and a young woman with long blonde hair in an oversized woollen jumper pushed through the door. She stopped short when she saw the policeman. She looked from Gerry to Dan. Her voice, cautious and uncertain, asked, 'What's going on?' Despite her dishevelled appearance, Dan could see that she was a good-looking girl and wondered idly what she was doing with the likes of Gerry.

'It's Sean,' Gerry started, '…he's been found dead in the street.'

Dan was struck by the lack of emotion in Gerry's voice.

The young woman stood motionless. Tears welled up in her blue eyes, and she stood fixed to the spot. Her hands, with their immaculately manicured nails, flew up to cover her mouth.

Dan stood and took in the scene. Over the years, he learned that he often discovered more by just quietly observing people. He noticed the look of irritation that passed over Gerry's face.

'Finula, get a grip. Sure, you hardly knew Sean, at least that's what you told *me*.' Gerry fired a meaningful look at the girl standing shivering, now with her arms wrapped around herself as if trying to contain her emotions.

Dan looked from one to the other, picking up on the tension between the young couple.

Finula took a deep, shuddering breath and, with a whimper, turned and ran back upstairs.

Gerry continued with the drying up, the glasses clinking as he placed them back on the shelves. His slow movements as he completed his mundane tasks grated on Dan's nerves. With a brief farewell, Dan exited the bar, relieved to be back outside in the fresh air and daylight.

***

Later that day, as another night shift loomed ahead, Dan focused on his first evening task. He needed to ask Deirdre a few questions. He had avoided questioning the young woman earlier due to the shock she must have had. She was a timid little thing, and he was doubtful that she was a crazed murderer.

'But you never know!' he reminded himself. He had many shocks himself over the years. It was the 'butter wouldn't melt in their mouth' type of people you had to watch.

But still, *Deirdre*?

So, more in line with following dutiful protocol than true suspicion, Dan stopped by Deirdre's tiny home on Scanlan Street to ask a few questions.

As he approached her front door, a little cat sat mewing, crying to get in. Deirdre had also heard the feline cries and opened the front door; a delighted look lit up her drawn face.

'*Patch!*' Deirdre gathered the fluffy bundle in her arms and was almost oblivious to Dan's presence on her doorstep.

Deirdre caught his eye over the ball of fluff and regained her composure. Remembering her manners, she ushered Dan into her humble home. The front door opened straight into the lounge. Deirdre indicated for Dan to take a seat as she sat cuddling the pet she thought was gone forever.

Dan, usually confident and relaxed around most people, felt awkward and ill at ease. The television was on full volume in the corner. Deirdre sat fussing with her cat. After Patch was welcomed back, his owner sat looking blankly at the ads on the television screen. Dan could no longer stand it; he took the initiative and switched the television off.

He cleared his throat and remarked that it had been a difficult day for Deirdre.

'Mmm,' Deirdre replied absently as Dan struggled to segue into his questions. He decided to go for the direct approach. 'Deirdre, I know you've had a terrible shock, but I must ask you. Where were you at 11 pm last night?'

'Sure, I was here, Dan,' she replied in a sing-song kind of voice that Dan found oddly unsettling.

'Were you alone?'

'Yes.' Deirdre continued to slowly stroke the appreciative Patch on his silky back. He responded with a throaty purr.

A muscle started to twitch in Dan's jaw. He was aware of it throbbing and also of his frustration levels rising. It had been a long day, and he hadn't slept much.

'Did you not wonder where Sean was all night?' Dan pressed, with more of an edge to his voice than he intended.

Deirdre looked up at him sharply and suddenly. She was looking at him straight in the eye with a confident intensity Dan had not seen in this young woman before.

'Wonder where he was?' She uttered the sentence more loudly than usual, with an impact not lost on Dan. Deirdre paused, her blank stare now replaced by hot anger. 'Sure, I've had plenty of practice. I'm always wondering where he is. I usually sit here on my own, night after night, with him out carousing. Last night was no different to any other night. I was here alone, nothing different there.'

Deirdre stood up with more assertion than Dan had ever seen her do anything in all the years he had known her.

'Good night, Dan. I'll be seeing you.' And with that, Deirdre took the few paces it took to reach the front door and opened it, letting in a blast of icy air.

After a few seconds, Dan stood up, touched his cap respectfully, and returned to the cold night. As Dan cycled into the night, he mused, 'What a fecking day it's been.' He murmured to himself, 'No further forward than I was hours ago.' Dan laboured slowly on the bike, feeling every one of his sixty years.

Chapter Eighteen

Was it Love?

Rosie was still reeling from the shock of Mary Jo's revelation regarding the malicious letter she had viewed that morning. Rosie felt drained, but she had promised to call to see Marie on the way home from work, and she had a plan. She was keen to see Marie. She wanted to get to know the young woman better and felt intensely uncomfortable about even considering her to have had a hand in Sean's demise. In all fairness, the solution was to befriend the newcomer and learn more about her. Rosie was also keen to see Deirdre, as she was concerned about this lonely girl spending such a difficult evening alone. The first night after the terrible news of the day. So, she planned to stop off at Marie's and see if she'd be up for a visit to Deirdre's. They could pick up some fish and chips on the way.

Marie was shutting up shop for the day and was just about to turn the door sign from 'open' to 'closed' when Rosie tapped the window, announcing her entrance. Marie opened the door eagerly, happy to see her new friend.

'Good to see you again, Rosie. How's your day been?' Marie asked politely. Marie had evidently composed herself since earlier in the day.

Marie's warm welcome tugged at Rosie's heart, and she felt terrible about her earlier suspicions.

'Well, you know how it is today. I've had better days, I'm sure,' Rosie replied truthfully. 'Now, Marie, I was thinking, would you mind coming with me to see Deirdre?'

Marie looked doubtful.

'Well, the thing is, I'm concerned about her and want to visit her, but I could do with a bit of moral support.' Rosie's plea was not entirely accurate, but she knew that appealing for help from someone like Marie, who seemed eager to please, would work.

'Of course.' Marie agreed without hesitation this time. Rosie had read Marie's character accurately, and her well-intentioned manipulations had worked.

'Right, so, now, have you eaten?' Without waiting for an answer, Rosie continued, 'We can get some fish and chips on the way. We pass the Penguin Fish Bar, so it won't take us out of our way. I'm sure Deirdre will be glad to have a bite to eat.' Ziggy gave a little bark in agreement.

'Sure, he recognises the words f-i-s-h and c-h-i-p-s!' Rosie spelt out the words to avoid further excitement on his part. With her plan now being executed, Rosie revived. She stood outside the shop with Ziggy while Marie locked up. While she waited, tapping her feet to keep warm, Rosie saw Sorcha lifting the curtain and looking out from her window above The Thatch. The image imprinted itself on Rosie's mind, and something clicked in her brain, but the moment passed as Marie joined her, keys jangling and her breath steaming in the cold night air.

'Okay, all ready, let's go.' The pair walked briskly along. Rosie linked arms with Marie, and Ziggy trotted along at Rosie's heels, ever hopeful of a share of fish and chips.

The trio arrived at Deirdre's door a short while later, dinner wrapped up in newspaper. The radio was on and the sad words of a slow ballad drifted out from behind the door.

Rosie and Marie glanced at each other and shrugged. Rosie tapped the door a little louder. The music stopped, and Deirdre appeared. The streetlight shone its eerie glow onto Deirdre's face.

Rosie stepped forward first. 'Deirdre, I'm so sorry for your loss, love. We've brought you a bit of dinner and thought you might like some company.'

Marie nodded warmly and smiled. Ziggy barked.

'Meow...'

Deirdre looked behind her as a vase got toppled over, and a furry flash indicated Patch had shot off through his cat flap in the back door.

'Hush, Ziggy!' Duly chastened, Ziggy was silenced, and he looked back at Rosie with hurt eyes as if to say, 'I was only saying hello!'

'Sorry, Deirdre, I forgot about the cat,' Rosie apologised.

'Never worry about him. Come in. Come in. Thanks for dinner. You're a star.' Deirdre welcomed her visitors in, relieved to have the company and something warm to eat.

Despite the circumstances, there was some laughter that night. Marie and Deirdre, closer in age than Rosie was to either of them, had a fair bit in common. Both women enjoyed reading, crafting, baking, and caring for animals. Deirdre listened, fascinated by Marie's stories of her life in London, especially some of the characters she met around Camden, where she ran a bookshop before coming to Ireland. Ziggy was absolved of his earlier indiscretion and entertained the ladies by jumping athletically and catching the chips they threw his way.

'Well, girls,' Rosie announced after a couple of hours. 'This has been great craic, but I need to move. I've got work in the morning.'

There were hugs all around, and they promised to catch up over the weekend.

Deirdre stood waving by her front door as Rosie, Marie, and Ziggy made their way homeward.

Marie, now feeling more relaxed in the company of her friend, ventured, 'Well, that was all very pleasant, but don't you think it was a bit odd?'

Rosie nodded. Marie did not need to continue. Over the whole course of the evening, Deirdre did not mention Sean's name. Not even once.

Now, that was indeed odd.

Chapter Nineteen

An Elevated View

Mary Jo slept on the top floor as the youngest and fittest of the Carmelite sisters in the Erin's Glen convent house. Known as 'Riverside House', the tall, white, shuttered building enjoyed a view of the usually tranquil river. Mary Jo had a long, thin room that benefitted from a dormer window on one end, overlooking the river and a skylight in the roof over her bed. Although slightly old-fashioned and spartan, the sloping roof and tiny iron fireplace in the corner gave the room a snug and homely feel.

When assigned her room on her arrival a few years previously, Mary Jo had quipped, 'Ah, great, I'll be closer to God up there!' The older sisters didn't laugh. Not all her sisters in Christ shared her sense of humour. Luckily, Mary Jo didn't mind the four-flight run up to her room. During daylight hours, she was rewarded with views from her window at the back of the house, over the river towards the hills and mountains behind. These provided an endless seasonal kaleidoscope of colour, outlines, and textures. She was close enough to the countryside in spring and summer to hear the lambs and sheep bleat up on the hills. The ever-changing panoply of stars and waxing and waning moon at bedtime blessed her with a cosmic focus during her nightly prayers. These simple sounds and sights of nature gave her an uncomplicated but profound joy.

This morning, Mary Jo woke up to the sound of the river Abanculeen, gushing loudly. There was the gentle pitter-patter of rain on the skylight above her bed. Upon waking, Mary Jo could sense that the intense cold of the previous few days had eased a little. She noticed that her breath was less apparent as a warm steam in the cold air of her bedroom. Central heating was not standard in Erin's Glen, and Riverside House was no exception. Thankful for the softer feel to the day, Mary Jo got up from her bed, determined to run now that it sounded like the snow had thawed. She dressed quickly in a T-shirt and thick brown tracksuit, tucked her greying light brown hair into a bandana, and was off. Mary Jo treaded lightly but quickly down the stairs. The large kitchen door was open, and some enticing warmth from the range by the far wall met her. After a quick glass of water and a bathroom visit, Mary Jo let herself quietly out the door and paused to enjoy her first breath of sweet morning air before the day started.

This was the time of day she loved best. Her brisk walking, which soon broke into a steady jog, gave her time to think. The small clock tower opposite Riverside House informed her that it was just after 6 am. It was still dark, and a solitary bright morning star punctured the inky sky. The snow and ice had given way to a wet slush, and Mary Jo could feel the cold dampness around her feet and ankles. Mary Jo focused on the problems presented by recent events partly to keep her mind off the less pleasant physical sensations of her run and partially to unravel the knot of puzzlement in her head. She mentally listed them: first, the odd letter that Father Gerard had received. Rosie had told her all about it, in confidence, of course. Second, Sean was found dead on the street yesterday morning. 'May his soul and all the souls of the faithful departed rest in peace,' she recited the short prayer as was her wish when speaking of the newly departed. She wasn't sure if 'faithful' applied to Sean, but she was genuinely disturbed by his death and sent a prayer up for him regardless. Number three on her list of current mysteries was the revelation she had yesterday in a meeting with her principal at the school.

While speaking with Miss McGrath, cloistered in her office yesterday after Dan had brought the news of Sean's death, the head teacher confided in Mary Jo that she had received a nasty letter. Mary Jo was shocked to learn that the letter sounded identical to the one Father Gerard had received. Rosie had told her word for word what his letter had said. Of course, Mary Jo did not tell her school superior about the priest's letter, as she respected Rosie's confidence.

So today, thoughts of these unpleasant developments rested heavily on her heart and mind. How to proceed for the best? The usual school routine, extra staff meetings, and conversations with concerned students and parents had left her worn-out last night. She had climbed the flights of stairs up to her room slowly and heavily yesterday evening and fallen into bed, exhausted. Today, her mind was fresher, and she mentally grappled with the various strands of recent events.

So many questions went through her mind: what had been the cause of Sean's death? Did he fall over in the snow and expire due to concussion and hypothermia? If he *was* murdered, who was responsible? Who sent those odious letters and why? Were all of these events connected? And if so, in what way? Had Sean sent the letters?

Mary Jo concluded that whoever sent the letters must be the same person. The content, mode, and communication style were the same. Also, all the letters were delivered by hand.

Mary Jo pondered on the links between the letters and Sean. Why would Sean suddenly start sending these letters? Perhaps Sean had been sending them for some reason known only to himself?

Perhaps his death would mean the end of these unwanted communications. Time will tell.

As Mary Jo completed her circuit around the town's environs, where there was a little streetlight, she turned back toward Riverside House. Being an early riser, she was responsible for starting the porridge on arriving at the convent dwelling. Mary Jo consciously redirected her attention to the scene around her and slowed down to a stop, her hands on her hips as she took in the background. Her eyes slid over the dark silhouette of the hills enclosing the town. The sky was clearing, and the light rain had stopped. The only sound was some gulls screeching overhead and the sound of rushing water as the river was thawing. Mary Jo took a few deep breaths and closed her eyes momentarily. When she opened them again, the light had shifted fractionally and revealed a sight that made Mary Jo gasp in surprise. And horror.

Chapter Twenty

Unwelcome News

Twenty-four hours previously, Jim Noonan had been tucking into a generous helping of cooked breakfast. His little eyes feasted on the large plate of bacon, sausages, black pudding, fried soda farls and potato bread complete with baked beans. A massive pot of tea sat in front of him.

He was just about to bite on a particularly succulent-looking sausage when a waiter hurried over to him, 'I'm sorry, sir, but there's a call for you.' Jim Noonan was not happy, and he made his feelings known to the waiter.

'Can't you see I'm eating, man!' he shouted. A bit of greasy egg slid down his chin.

The waiter politely ignored Jim's appearance and reaction and whispered, 'It's the police, sir.' Jim rose from his chair with a sigh, pulling his bib-like napkin away from his shirtfront and wiping away the egg. The fastidious waiter looked relieved and smiled wanly.

'Thank you, sir, this way, sir.'

Jim followed the staff member to the reception desk, picking up the phone, 'Jim here, what is it?'

As Jim absorbed the news communicated to him over the phone, his irritated expression transfigured into a look of shock. His skin visibly paled. Jim Noonan loved his food, but on finishing the short call, he put the phone down slowly and bypassed the dining room. He had suddenly lost his appetite.

Jim quickly gathered his few belongings from his hotel room and checked out. Before doing so, he had quickly called The Thatch to check on the pub. Katie sounded like she was in shock herself but reassured him that nothing else was amiss. He mused on how bad this would be for business. God help him when the local rag, *The Erin's Glen Herald*, got a hold of this story. He could see the headlines: 'Publican's Cousin Found Dead Outside Bar'. That numpty who ran Shenanigans would be having a field day.

Such were the thoughts running through Jim Noonan's head as Jim started the drive home in the snow. The tractors had cleared some of it, but the exposed bits of tarmac were icing over quickly. Thick snow was banked up along the sides of the winding roads. Jim wanted to race back to Erin's Glen but felt compelled by the road conditions to keep his foot close to the brake.

As Jim, Marie, Rosie, and the other residents of Erin's Glen absorbed the shocking news of that morning, Father Gerard sat in his church. As yet, he was unaware of the events in the town – unaware that he would shortly have a funeral to conduct. Oblivious to this despicable deed, his mind was on his recently received message. He had decided to ignore the note and see what might happen. Perhaps it was a one-off occurrence. Some in his parish intensely disliked the church and its clerics. Maybe this was a critique of the church in general. Perhaps he was taking the contents of the note too personally. Thus mollified, he decided to keep it to himself, and he would ask Rosie to do the same.

He sat in silence for a few minutes. The stillness of the church at this time of the early morning was a source of comfort to him. He was vaguely aware of the clock ticking at the back of the church. The sounds of birds' whistles echoed through the porch. In the far distance was the sound of early lambs bleating, looking for their mothers on the hillside.

Suddenly, the silence was broken by a heavy metallic clunk. Instinctively, Father Gerard looked behind him as he stayed seated on the pew. The massive handle on the church door had turned, and the wide wooden door creaked open.

Father Gerard had a visitor.

Chapter Twenty-One

Back Stories

The morning after visiting Deirdre, Marie felt more at home in her new abode than anywhere in a long time. Despite the distressing events of the day before, Marie now felt part of the community. She mused on how difficult circumstances often bring people together, which was undoubtedly her recent experience.

Rosie's request to join her to support Deirdre the previous evening helped Marie feel more involved. It drew her into the close-knit circle of friends, neighbours, and family that made up Erin's Glen. Upon waking, Marie took a few moments to reflect on these positive emotions before braving the cold morning and throwing back her patchwork quilt. She threw a chunky Aran cardigan over her pyjamas and slid her feet into furry slippers. Feeling sleepy but content, she shuffled drowsily to her kitchen to make tea.

The elusive Willow had disappeared again last night, and Marie hoped he would turn up soon looking for his breakfast. Just as she had that thought, he appeared on cue, glaring accusingly at her through her kitchen window. The feline gymnast had shimmied his way up a network of pipes and gutters and used a series of roofs on the extended building below to make his way up to the source of his breakfast.

'Ah, Willow, you clever boy!' Marie welcomed her new pet inside as she opened the window.

He pounced in gracefully and wound himself around her ankles as she scraped a tin of sardines onto a saucer for him.

'Don't get too used to this, matey. Once I can go to the shops, you'll be on the Whiskas.'

Marie opened the fridge and realised she was out of milk. As Willow tucked into his smelly fish dish, Marie skipped downstairs to her front door to fetch the milk bottle the milkman would have delivered earlier that morning. As she stooped to pick it up, a doll with long purple hair got thrust in her face.

'Hello, Roisin!' Marie greeted the owner of the doll warmly.

'For goodness' sake, Roisin, don't stick that doll in people's faces!' Roisin's mother, Trish, scolded her daughter, then quickly switched her attention to Marie. 'Good morning, Marie. How are you doing?' Without waiting for a reply, Trish said, 'I'll catch up with you later when I've dropped this munchkin off at school.' Trish clearly wanted to chat with Marie, but not in front of her little daughter. Marie got her drift. No doubt Trish felt the urge to share her thoughts on the previous day's events but didn't want to discuss the grisly details in the young girl's hearing.

'Okay, no worries, see you later. Bye Roisin, nice to see you and Sandra again!' Marie waved as the pair hurried off down the street.

Roisin waved back, delighted that this new lady had remembered the name of her dolly.

A short while later, after Marie had breakfasted on a simple meal of tea and toast, she returned downstairs to the shop and proceeded to open up for the day. She took the opportunity to step outside and look at her shopfront from the street. She was pleased with her window display with its pink and red hearts hanging down on ribbons from the ceiling, pink cloth lining the window floor, and romance-themed books arranged attractively amid some sparkling confetti. Marie frowned as she looked up at the shop sign. She still needed a signwriter to change the proprietor's name:

'Will Flynn Books and Stationery Supplies'.

Marie wanted a catchier title than that. One with a bit more imaginative flair, but she couldn't think what it should be. Somehow, 'Marie Miller Books' didn't tick the boxes. So, until she decided what the sign would change to, the difficulty of getting a signwriter was irrelevant anyway.

Marie wasn't long back in the shop when Trish O'Hara returned.

'Ah, great to get a chance to talk to you, Marie. How are you settling in?' Trish settled herself down on the shabby, dark red armchair intended for customers who wanted to linger.

'Fine, everyone's been very friendly,' Marie had just started to express her thoughts when Trish broke in, obviously more accustomed to quicker speakers.

'Well, whoever did Sean in wasn't very friendly. I hope it hasn't put you off, but he was an oddball, never fitted in, a malcontent, you know what I mean?'

Marie realised all she needed to do was nod to keep the flow going.

Trish continued, 'His father, Will, owned this place.' Marie was aware of this but kept nodding, sure that this information was just a warm-up for juicier stuff. 'Well, he owned half of Erin's Glen. A strange business him just taking off after the fire.'

All Marie needed to do was incline her head to one side with a quizzical expression; this gave Trish a licence to carry on. 'There was a big fire up at the car workshop. Nearly burnt to the ground, it was. And old Will disappeared after that. Sean built it up a bit, but it was never the same. I heard there was no insurance money, so to give Sean his due, he had it tough, I suppose.' Trish took a nano-second to reflect on this. 'But anyway, that was years ago. I suppose old Will has been presumed dead.' At this point, it was clear from Trish's unaccustomed pause that she was looking to Marie for confirmation of this presumed titbit of information.

Marie confirmed that it was her understanding that Will was dead.

'Ah, right so. Strange business through all that. Old Will would be in his eighties now. He had Sean late in life, you know.' Trish appeared satisfied with this exchange of information. And so, obviously feeling that her mission had been accomplished, she stood up. Wrapping her coat tighter around her ample frame, she gushed, 'Well, you've done a grand job, a grand job.' Trish then trotted off to her hair and beauty salon with this parting expression of effusive praise and appreciation.

Chapter Twenty-Two

A Riverside Discovery

Marie and Trish were blissfully unaware of the dramatic events earlier that morning. If they had known of the following unfortunate incident to occur in their small town, they would probably have lingered longer in their conversation.

That same morning, Mary Jo had woken up with the urge to exercise before the day started. Luckily, she had decided to go for a run despite the freezing slush that the thawing snow had turned into. It was also fortuitous that she was an early riser.

Mary Jo had completed a circuit around the environs of the town. She jogged up along Rainbow Row towards the dark silhouette of Slieve Cairn. The sky was still dark, and one star glittered above the mountain's peak. Constrained by the need to stay within the orange glow of the streetlights on the dark winter's morning, Mary Jo circled round back down the opposite side of the street towards the river. Being a fit and frequent runner, she found the short route was simply a refreshing start to the day. Her exertions had left her feeling revitalised and energised, and her body was warm from the movement. The air felt cool and fresh on her face, and she slowed down to fully appreciate the morning. The gushing river was close, and Mary Jo could hear its gurgling and glugging as she drew nearer. Coming to the end of her short run, she glanced at the river Abanculeen; the water was high this morning due to the overnight thaw.

She took a double take as she caught sight of an Ophelia-like figure lying face up in the water. The soft glow from the streetlight created a luminous gleam on the pale face, hallowed by weedy strands of long, light-coloured hair. The river tugged at the body, willing it to travel onwards on its journey to the sea, but an item of clothing had got caught on some rocks and held the body captive to the bank.

Mary Jo, an accomplished swimmer, took no hesitation in pulling off her thick tracksuit top in hasty preparation for an unplanned dip. She ran the short distance to the river and waded in, gasping with shock at the bone-chilling cold of the water, even though it only reached her armpits. The strong current tugged at her legs; its fierceness might have undermined a less experienced swimmer, but Mary Jo held her nerve and strode out confidently. She managed to get hold of an arm and tugged desperately; she heard the sound of cloth tearing and nearly fell back into the water as the body was released from its moorings. Mary Jo righted herself and bobbled back up again. Keeping a firm hold under each arm, she heaved the body, clothed in a thick, water-logged coat and boots, up onto dry land, reaching a flatter area by the side of the river. As a physical education teacher, Mary Jo was well trained in the basics of first aid and immediately turned the person onto their side in a recovery position, thumping their back to get a response and starting to expel water from the lungs.

While performing her first aid drill, she saw that it was Deirdre she was dealing with. There was no time for pondering now. Mary

Jo knew she needed to act quickly. As she examined Deirdre rapidly, it was a relief to her to detect a pulse and a faint, warm breath. The young woman lay on the bank, eyes closed and breathing shallowly. Satisfied that Deirdre was out of immediate danger, the nun ran back, picked up her thick tracksuit top that she had discarded in her race to the rescue and placed it over Deirdre. Mary Jo was aware of her own thudding heart pounding in her chest. Her breaths were rapid and gasping, resulting from a combination of shock, cold and fast physical exertion. With no time for reflection, Mary Jo turned towards Riverside House and ran in through the unlocked door. The phone, being located in the hallway, was within easy reach. An ambulance was summoned, and Mary Jo returned to the patient. Deirdre lay, a limp, wet, bedraggled creature in a sopping woollen coat. She was breathing but unresponsive to Mary Jo's voice. Mary Jo crouched by her side, stoking her wet hair and speaking to her soothingly.

After what seemed like an eternity but was, in fact, just a few minutes, an ambulance trundled up the deserted street. It crept swiftly along without a siren or flashing lights at this early hour. Mary Jo watched as the vehicle moved up and over the little bridge and parked by the sloping bank, which parents usually occupied with young children feeding the ducks. The two male, middle-aged ambulance crew, who had been on standby all night, jumped out – quickly assessing the situation, they grabbed a stretcher and warm blankets, draping one over the now-shivering Mary Jo and the patient.

After a brief exchange of questions and answers to ascertain the rescuer's and patient's circumstances and identity, Deirdre was taken off safely to the warmth of the cottage hospital. Mary Jo had declined the invitation to visit the hospital herself for a check-up, dismissing the suggestion with a light laugh and a wave of her hand. No need, she had assured them. She'd only been in the water a few seconds. She'd been in colder water than that whilst completing her triathlons in Tralee. Watching the ambulance turn the corner at the end of the street, Mary Jo returned to Riverside House. As she re-entered the house for the second time that morning, a bewildered Sister Angela was descending the stairs slowly.

'In God's name...' She started to exclaim as she saw her soaked convent sister returning home with a blanket around her shoulders. 'What on earth have you been doing?'

The elderly sisters were used to their junior sister's fitness fads, everything from long-distance running to wild swimming, so Sister Angela was only mildly surprised to see Mary Jo in such a state. Only when the younger nun requested some extra strong tea with a nip of brandy from the first aid box did Sister Angela realise something was amiss.

Mary Jo stopped shivering after a hot bath and a steaming cup of fortified tea and could recount her morning exploits. Sister Angela sat alongside her heroic companion by the range in the large kitchen. They both pondered on what could have been the story behind Deirdre's dramatic appearance in the river. 'Had she fallen in, and if so, why was she out at such an early hour? Had she been pushed into the swollen river, and if so, by whom? Was this occurrence linked to Sean's death, and how?'

Sister Angela and Mary Jo shook their heads sadly. What on earth was going on in Erin's Glen?

Chapter Twenty-Three

A Gloomy Day

Many of the residents of Erin's Glen, unaccustomed to such concentrated drama, went about their daily routines in shock. The weekend beckoned, and all hoped there would be a respite from the circulating lousy news. The rumour mill was in full swing.

Mary Jo insisted on going to school as usual. She dismissed her morning heroics as nothing more than an early dip. Sister Angela was not convinced but knew how stubborn her junior sister was, so she backed down, and Mary Jo whisked off to school as if nothing had happened. On arrival at school, she spoke with a stunned Miss Grath to explain Deirdre's absence. Deirdre's immediate supervisor, Maggie, the cook, was also informed but with a heavily edited version of events. Maggie was not surprised by Deirdre's absence and accepted Mary Jo's explanation of Deirdre needing some time to recover from the shock as perfectly plausible. Mary Jo knew gossip would be rife in town, and she wanted to spare Deirdre the embarrassment of being at the centre of it, so she kept the conversation short and the details sketchy.

The nun was keen to discuss the situation with her friend, Rosie. Events were overtaking them fast, and they needed to get their heads together to figure out what was happening. So, before lessons began, Mary Jo quickly called Rosie to arrange an afternoon visit. She promptly told Rosie about her morning's rescue without going into details. With so much to mull over, Mary Jo and Rosie felt the need to take stock in Rosie's bungalow up the hill; with an afternoon get-together organised, Mary Jo continued her lessons and somehow got through the day. She was even more heartened to know that the meeting would include tea, homemade scones, and cake.

Rosie was equally looking forward to the meeting later that day. It always helped her to clarify her thoughts and impressions with her trusted friend. She would have enough time to finish work at 1 pm, get home, give Ziggy a quick walk and get the scones and cake into the oven before her friend arrived at 4 pm. Rosie decided to make her special lemon drizzle cake as a treat to cheer themselves up. Only the day before, she had been reading in her *Women's World* magazine about how cheering citrus fruits were so that the cake would be virtually medicinal; she convinced herself. With her day neatly mapped out in her head, Rosie got on with her jobs in the parish office. She had the parish newsletter to type up and entries to make in the book of parish records.

The day was dull and overcast, and the office seemed darker than usual. Rosie switched on the lights and immediately became aware of the shrouded box-like shape that loomed in the corner. This was the new computer that had been delivered a few months before. This also worried Rosie. What was wrong with her old, reliable Olivetti typewriter? She was due to go on some Diocesan training later in the year, which filled her with dread. She had avoided all invitations to IT training so far, and thankfully, Father Gerard didn't put any pressure on her.

When she read the leaflet about the IT training coming up, she was none the wiser. It was like a different language. As far as she was concerned, 'windows' were for looking out of to enjoy a view. She couldn't understand what they had to do with computers. Not keen on small rodents, she was also unsettled by references to 'a mouse'. She had unpacked the computer herself and not found any little furry creatures in the box. It was all very confusing. The printer that came with it was even more of a mystery. She didn't know a daisy wheel from a daisy chain. She was still getting to grips with the photocopier and fax, now a printer to contend with. It was all too much. Perhaps she could eke out another year or two in her post before retirement and avoid dealing with the shrouded horror in the corner.

The computer wasn't the only thing making her feel unsettled. Father Gerard, usually cheerful and chatty, appeared distant and distracted these past few days. She resolved to speak with him to find out what was happening. As if on cue, Father Gerard came into the office, looking older than his years and slightly stooped; Rosie felt a rush of concern and affection for this man, who she had always known to be conscientious and kind.

After discussing a few dates for upcoming baptisms and arrangements to be made, Rosie asked if she could have a word. Father Gerard immediately looked concerned about her and sat down, asking, 'What is it, Rosie?' They had known each other for most of their lives. They knew nearly everybody in Erin's Glen and had a long and rich shared history.

Despite her familiarity on a personal level, Rosie had always tried to be professional in her role as secretary to the parish priest. She respected boundaries and knew when to ask questions and be quiet.

But today, she felt compelled to step away from her work role and put the same questions to him. She looked him straight in the face, sitting opposite her on an office chair. 'Gerard,' she began, dropping the 'Father' as she addressed him as a friend. A slight inflexion on his part showed that he registered her intention. 'Gerard, I'm currently worried about so many things going on in Erin's Glen.' He continued to watch her face patiently and intently. 'I'm concerned about what happened to Sean. It's so sad that his young life was cut short. And just this morning, I heard Deirdre was rescued half-drowned from the river. It's a terrible turn of events and all so worrying.'

Father Gerard was very much in agreement with her. Sister Angela had already been on the phone to him about the drama involving Deirdre that morning, so this latest development was not news to him. He had known both Sean and Deirdre since they were babies and was very distressed about these events. He took a deep sigh, indicating his feelings.

Rosie went on, 'I'm worried about you too, Gerard. You're not yourself at all. You've hardly spoken a word to me these past few days, and there's been those awful letters. What does it all mean?'

'Aye. Those letters...' Father Gerard sighed deeply before continuing. 'There's been a development. Whoever has been putting these letters together has moved on to attempting to blackmail me.'

'Blackmail?' Rosie managed to squeak. 'Who on earth would be blackmailing you? And why?'

Gerard took a deep breath, put his head back onto the neck rest on the high-backed office chair and considered what he would say next.

What he shared with Rosie rocked her view of her little world, Erin's Glen.

Chapter Twenty-Four

Taking Stock

Marie was looking forward to a quiet weekend. She had grown accustomed to the gentle rhythm of her days in Erin's Glen, and recent events had shaken her, too. However, she had a shop to run and was busy ordering stationery and art supplies, pricing up stock and doing accounts in between serving customers. As a shopkeeper with contact with many people in the community, she was getting used to the many questions and leading comments she would get from customers, looking for gossip. She did her best to field most of them off with evasive answers. She felt something was happening with Deirdre but didn't know what. Quite a few customers asked about her welfare, commenting that she wasn't at work that day. No doubt Maggie, the cook, had put her feelers out to get more details about Deirdre's absence. Just as Marie was musing on this, Mary Jo swept into the shop with her customary bustle.

'I've just popped in to see how you're doing.' Mary Jo looked at Marie with her twinkly blue eyes. Her face was ruddy, from the cold air.

Marie paused and affirmed that she was well but concerned about Deirdre due to the questions she was getting from customers.

'Well, that's another reason I popped in, to be honest.'

Marie watched Mary Jo intently as she outlined the events of that morning. Her face registered concern about her new friend.

'Rosie was telling me you and Deirdre have hit it off. You certainly seemed to have a lot in common when we had our craft night in the week.' Mary Jo smiled and continued, 'I was wondering if you could pop over to the cottage hospital to see her? She will be alone over there, and I am sure it would cheer her up no end to see you.'

Marie affirmed that she would as soon as she closed up the shop that evening. Duly reassured, Mary Jo carried on her way up the hill to see Rosie and hopefully try to make some sense of recent events.

After the whirlwind Mary Jo left, the shop felt eerily quiet. The days were still short, and the darkness was creeping in early. Marie felt a chill creep over her. She shivered and pulled on her Aran cardigan draped over the back of the armchair. She hugged herself tight as she went into her little kitchenette to make a warming brew. She seemed to have become a tea drinker now and smiled as she reflected on how she had been seemingly brainwashed into this change of beverage choice.

She took a moment to sit in the large red armchair, cradling her mug of tea in her hands and feeling cosier in her thick woollen cardigan. Her gaze settled on the view outside her window; she could see lights on in the room above the bar in The Thatch. Above that, she could see a strip of sky just starting to darken, a few wisps of orange in the sky from the weak sun that was setting. Lulled by the comfortable seat, warm drink, and sombre sky, Marie's thoughts drifted to how much her life had changed in recent weeks. With one hand holding her tea, she reached up to the necklace she always wore these days and touched it, winding the chain around her fingers as she thought back over recent months. Erin's Glen was a world away from her old life in Camden. She had stocked pop and rock T-shirts, comic books, and music memorabilia in her trendy London bookshop. It had none of the quaint charm that she was enjoying here. Marie smiled gently; despite the troubling events in Erin's Glen, she felt more settled and contented here than she had in a long time.

The road to her arrival in this overlooked but picturesque glen was long and winding. She reflected again on her mother's illness. After her father had already passed away, and she found herself alone dealing with her mother, life had become increasingly difficult. Her mother had grown more confused and forgetful with each passing day. Initially, Marie had thought that her mother's failing memory and bewilderment were due to grief and loneliness. Still, as the months went on, it became apparent that her mental faculties would not improve with time or adjustment to life on her own.

Eventually, after many assessments and visits to the hospital, her mother, Nancy, was diagnosed with Alzheimer's. Marie was advised to find a care home for Nancy. This involved many trips to various specialist units and meetings with solicitors and banks to arrange Power of Attorney to enable Marie to deal with her mother's finances and make arrangements for her care. Marie had to fit these filial duties around her business, and the stress involved in keeping her business going, caring for her mother, and making plans for her future was tremendous.

Not least on the list of stresses was dealing with her mother's possessions. A tall, four-storey Victorian terrace in North London had been the family home. Of course, Marie had moved out years ago into her own flat, but the house seemed to get more cluttered after her departure. On her frequent visits to see her mum, Marie would make valiant efforts to clear out unneeded items from the house. Nancy was particularly possessive about her bedroom and made it clear to Marie that this was a no-go area, which Marie respected. However, after Nancy moved into The Farringdon House Care Home, Marie set about cleaning out even this inner sanctum. The house needed to be sold, and due to necessity, no part of the house was now out of bounds.

What Marie discovered in a shoebox in the deepest recesses of the wardrobe in the room her mother and father shared changed Marie's life and led her here to Erin's Glen.

Marie was propelled out of her late afternoon ruminations by the shop bell jangling. It was Trish O'Hara back with the latest instalment of news from the day. She spoke in hushed whispers as Roisin, her little daughter, stood behind her.

'Did you hear, Marie, about Deirdre, found in the...' Trish mouthed the word: *river* '...this morning.'

It was just as well Marie did know something of the event as Trish, in her efforts to keep the story's full impact out of her daughter's hearing, was hardly audible.

Marie nodded, and Trish continued in a hushed whisper, 'I feel terribly sorry for that poor girl. You know Sean was carrying on with that Katie from the bar? I've never had much time for Sean; sorry to speak ill of the dead, but he was trouble with a capital 'T'.'

Marie was just about to ask Trish how she knew about Sean and Katie's affair, but then again, Marie had been in Erin's Glen long enough to know that keeping secrets, especially from hairdressers, was hard.

Trish turned back to check on Roisin and, seeing her look out of the shop window, gazing up at the illuminated window across the street, scolded Roisin for being nosey. 'I've told you before not to be staring over at that poor critter!' Looking at a nonplussed Marie, she exclaimed, 'What's she like? I don't know where she gets it from!'

And with that, Trish swept out the door. The irony of the situation completely lost on her.

Chapter Twenty-Five

A Letter from Angel Hill

Marie still had that letter. The letter that had changed her understanding of her identity and where she had come from. Marie was looking at it now. It was neatly folded in its original envelope and addressed to her parents, Mr and Mrs Richard Miller.

As Marie carefully lifted the delicate letter, worn thin with age, a silver chain with a medal-shaped pendant slithered out from its folds. It fell, twinkling onto the bedcovers. Marie inspected it closely. It had a heart shape on one side, made up of an intertwined, loopy pattern with a green stone in the middle; she turned it over and read the initials written on the reverse: M.A.M. '*Mam?*' Marie queried to herself. Or perhaps her initials: Marie Anne Miller?

Marie put the necklace to one side and returned her attention to the letter. By now, over forty years on, it was discoloured and felt fragile to the touch. Marie looked again at the letter as she sat crossed-legged on her big soft bed under the eaves upstairs from her bookshop in Erin's Glen. Its contents had taken her back to the beginning of the quest that had brought her to this quaint little backwater. She reread the words that had shaken her to the core a couple of years before when she was clearing out the wardrobe in her mother's bedroom in preparation for the house sale.

As she unfolded the yellowed paper, it sent out a musty scent that took her right back to the first time she had read those fateful words, words that were etched in her memory. Although she had memorised its contents, she reread the beautiful handwritten script:

Dear Mr and Mrs Miller

Thank you for your recent enquiry about possibly adopting a child.

I am delighted to inform you that a young female child, only a few weeks old, has come into our care. Her mother is a young girl from Ireland, too young to take adequate care of the child. The mother is well-educated and from a good family.

Therefore, I invite you to meet the baby at the Angel Hill Convent. We can make the necessary arrangements if you want to adopt the child.

I look forward to hearing back from you on your thoughts on this matter.

Yours sincerely

Sister Anthony

The letterhead stated that the letter was from 'The Sisters of Charity, Angel Hill Convent' with an address in North London, close to where Marie lived in her London flat when she discovered the letter.

At first, due to shock and denial, Marie had assumed the letter did not concern her. At times in her childhood and teenage years, she had felt quite different from her parents. But all youngsters experienced these types of feelings, didn't they? Perhaps due to adolescent rebellion or asserting one's own personality? These feelings were a normal part of growing up, weren't they?

However, as Marie considered the letter's contents, her heartbeat quickened, and her palms grew sweaty. She was unsettled by her discovery and decided to investigate further. What *had* been going on in the family? Perhaps her parents had considered adopting a child, but then she had come along. She had heard cases like this; would-be hopeful parents had given up on having their child, and they had conceived whilst pursuing other options, and the unexpected had happened. But Marie knew in her heart that this was probably not the case. Her mother had never discussed a pregnancy. There were no photos of Marie as a newborn or images of her mother looking pregnant. Her mother had looked consistently pencil-thin in the old black-and-white photographs from the 1950s and 1960s.

To compound matters, the Millers had been an insular family. There was no extended network of aunts, uncles, or cousins, and Marie had no siblings. She was vaguely aware of older family members who had died in the London Blitz during the Second World War, so the impact of the war had decimated the family. There were no other older kin to question. Marie's heart sank at the prospect of getting any sense out of Nancy, her mother. However, she resolved to ask her mother when she was in one of her more lucid moments.

After discovering the letter, Marie was relieved to see her mother sitting in an armchair downstairs on her next visit to the Farringdon nursing home. That was always a good sign. Marie walked hopefully towards her mother, seated amongst the palms in the conservatory. She looked pretty perky, with a crossword in her lap and smiled warmly as Marie approached her. Her cold, thin hands reached to cup Marie's face as she bent down to peck her mum on the cheek.

After a few pleasantries, Marie pulled her chair closer to her mother's. 'Mum, I need to ask you something.'

Marie wasn't quite sure how to continue. Her mother nodded, eyebrows raised; her eyes looked faded and red-rimmed. 'Yes, dear. What is it?'

Marie opened and closed her mouth and, with frustration, felt hot tears well up in her eyes.

Seeing her distress, her mother leaned forward, closed her misshapen, bony hands over Marie's, and waited.

Wordlessly, Marie removed her hands from her mother's and produced the letter she had found. Her mother's eyes were fixed on it. Nancy paused with a frown. After a short intake of breath, she remarked, 'I told you. You know all about this.'

'What do you mean, *I know*?' Marie was quite sure this was news to her.

'But darling, your father and I told you when you were tiny. We didn't want to make a whole song and dance, so we never mentioned it again. You were our little girl, and we loved you – I still love you; that's all that matters, surely?'

While saying these words, Nancy waved her hands about expansively, smiling and shrugging her shoulders. Her tone was light-hearted and merry.

Marie remained stonily silent.

'It was so long ago...' Nancy made a last effort to dismiss Marie's questions. They both sat sad and distanced from each other by misunderstandings, time, and vastly different views.

Marie looked back at her mother blankly. She gritted her teeth with rage and incomprehension. 'No, Mum, I didn't know.'

After a few moments, Nancy suddenly looked exhausted and skinny in the massive high-backed chair. Her face drained of colour, and she seemed to retreat back into her own world. Nancy began fiddling with her crossword and pencil, eyes drifting back to the puzzle. An annoying habit her mother had when she wanted to avoid any form of confrontation.

Marie needed to get out from the cloying warmth of the conservatory. It felt like everything was telescoping inwards. Everything she thought she knew and understood about her life was turned upside down. If she wasn't Marie Miller, only child; Mother, Nancy Miller née Wilson, and Father, Richard Miller from Surrey, then who was she?

She stood up abruptly and walked away. Looking back at Nancy's slumped figure, she could see that she had returned her attention to the puzzle on her lap. Marie was left now with her own mystery to solve.

The mystery of who she was – who she *is*.

That evening, she sat staring into the mirror, the letter in her hands. She spent a long time looking at her familiar reflection. She searched her grey-green eyes, scanning her face with its fair skin and a light sprinkling of freckles and examining her brown hair that flashed auburn in the right light. Who was she?

Marie was determined to find out.

Chapter Twenty-Six

A Visit to Angel Hill

After Marie's unsatisfactory attempt to find out the details of her origins from her mother, she decided to visit the convent Angel Hill, which was just a short bus ride away. Marie doubted that any of the original sisters would still be there, but someone could look up some records for her.

Before hopping on a bus to visit the convent, she had made a phone call to arrange an appointment. She had spoken with a friendly-sounding woman who told Marie to pop around during office hours whenever she was in the area.

She had the letter safely stowed inside her shoulder bag and approached the convent house with trepidation. Marie was aware of her thudding heart as she made her way past the large rhododendron bush that the drive swirled around.

Her destination was tucked away behind some tall gates. The narrow, meandering driveway led up to a wide double-fronted house of two storeys. It looked like it had been recently refurbished; the plastering, window frames, and fascia appeared freshly painted.

The heavy outer front door was propped open, and Marie stepped into a small porchway. The inner door shot open quickly, and Marie was welcomed into a large hallway by a tall, slim woman with beautiful ebony-coloured skin, a captivating smile, and flashing eyes. She wore a habit indicating she was a Sister of Charity.

'Come in. Is it Marie?'

Marie nodded.

'I'm Sister Marion. Would you like some tea?'

Marie doubted she could hold a cup of tea without spilling it due to nerves. So, she thought it safer to decline the offer.

'As you wish. Let's go through to the office and have a chat then.' Sister Marion led the way down the hallway, the floor decorated with ornate Victorian tiles. The office was housed down a few steps into an area of the building that looked like a modern extension. A large desk with a computer dominated the small room. Sister Marion sat behind the desk and reached for the letter Marie had extracted from her bag, peering at it through some reading glasses. Without a word, she swung around on her office chair and began rifling through the drawers of a tall filing cabinet behind her. Marie sat, perched on the edge of her chair, holding her breath, tense with anxiety.

Sister Marion closed the drawer, frowning; she rechecked the letter and opened another drawer. Marie struggled to sit patiently; she wanted to pull the nun out of the way and dive into those drawers herself. Resisting this impulse, she took a deep breath and waited, biting her lip nervously.

Sister Marion popped back up from her inspection of the lowest drawer and sighed. She produced a key hanging by her side and locked the filing cabinet.

'Sorry, we don't have the matching record for that date.'

Marie looked at her incredulously.

'There was a fire way back before I came here. Many of the older records were destroyed. That's why I'm trying to get them all onto the system.' Sister Marion pointed at the computer with a smile. Sensing Marie's deep disappointment, the nun cupped her chin thoughtfully. Her eyes lit up.

'I know, we can ask Sister Perpetua. She has been here forever! She might remember something. Just give me a moment.'

Sister Marion stalked gracefully out of the office, and Marie could hear her footsteps disappear back up the tiled hallway.

A range of emotions flashed across Marie's consciousness as she waited. Frustration and a sense of powerlessness dominated her feelings at that moment. Before she had time to reflect long on her disappointment, she heard the footsteps return as a quick tap-tap back along the hall. Marie stood up in preparation for the nun's return.

Sister Marion popped her head around the door; she waved her fingers at Marie, indicating to Marie for her to follow her. Marie clunked up the hall in her heavy boots after the nun and was ushered into a vast lounge with a bay window. As Marie gazed around, she almost missed a tiny, shrivelled figure sitting in a wheelchair. A tinkly, high-pitched voice greeted her.

'Hello, dear.' The little bundle of sticks thrust a brown-speckled hand out to Marie.

'Sister Perpetua.' And with that brief introduction, the statuesque Sister Marion left the room.

The older nun patted the seat of an armchair next to her. 'Come and take a seat, dear. I imagine you must be feeling rather nervous about all this. Tell me what you know, and I'll see if I can help you.' The little lady smiled and clasped her withered old hands in front of her on her lap. Marie felt reassured by her calm and patient composure and relaxed a little.

'Well, I have this letter.' Marie dived into her bag and retrieved it, handing it to the sister, who adjusted her glasses to inspect the letter.

'Thank you.' Sister Perpetua gently took the letter and held it delicately between her fingers, her lips moving slightly as she read the words with a serious expression of studied concentration.

She placed the letter in her lap, closed her eyes, and moved her head back a little. Marie sat patiently, hoping that the little nun would remember something.

'Ah, yes. I do remember this case.' Sister Perpetua held up a gnarled forefinger to add emphasis to her remembrance. 'Yes, it was a young woman from Ireland. A bit of a sorry tale about a romance she had thought would lead to marriage, but then so many did...'

Marie nodded encouragingly. This was not totally new information, and she was keen for the nun to continue her recollections. Marie unclasped the necklace from around her neck and showed it to Sister Perpetua to aid her in her efforts to cast her memory back all those decades ago.

'I found this with the letter,' Marie explained. 'I don't know if it is significant, but it might help you remember?'

Sister Perpetua leaned forward and draped the chain over her hands, cupping the pendant in her palm; she inspected it closely, frowning and turning it over.

'Yes, this rings a bell... ah, I remember now. The mother had an identical necklace. A Celtic heart of infinity on one side with an emerald...' Sister Perpetua turned the pendant over carefully. 'Yes, initials, 'M.A.M...' Sister Perpetua was silent for a few minutes, her eyes looking back into the distant past. After a minute, she tutted, shook her head, and sighed in frustration, 'Oh, I can't remember the name...'

Marie was prepared for disappointment. It was a long shot, but she had tried. All ready to receive her property back from the nun and make a polite departure, Sister Perpetua suddenly clapped her hands together. With more volume and power in her voice than Marie had thought possible, she almost shouted, 'Erin's Glen!'

Marie looked at her blankly.

'That's where the mother was from, Erin's Glen in Ireland. That is the only detail I remember. It was the necklace that brought the memory back. Does that help?' Sister Perpetua leaned forward and smiled enquiringly.

On impulse, Marie hugged her.

'Yes, yes, it does. Thank you so much. So, I must go to Erin's Glen to find my mother.'

And that is precisely what she did.

Chapter Twenty-Seven

Curls and Clues

Later that morning, Rosie made her way along Rainbow Row towards O'Hara's Hair and Beauty; she had her once-a-month appointment with Trish. Vanity was not Rosie's motivation but rather the desire to pick up any little titbits of information. A visit to the local hairdressers was usually fruitful. A blast of hot air hit Rosie as she stepped inside the door of the salon, the loud tinkle of the bell heralding her arrival. The sticky heat, thick with the whiff of chemicals, contrasted with the sharp, icy wind at her back as she entered. For a split second, the loud chatter stopped as the familiar faces paused mid-sentence to register the latest arrival that morning.

'Ah, there she is herself – morning, Rosie.' Trish O'Hara, the proprietor of O'Hara's Hair and Beauty, welcomed her regular customer warmly. Although not prone to paranoia, Rosie had the distinct impression she had been the subject of the chatter she had just interrupted.

Trish, quick as a flash, took Rosie's coat and enveloped her in a black cape, settling her in a salon chair in front of the mirror. Smiling at Rosie's reflection, she asked, 'Usual trim and tint, Rosie?'

'Thanks, that would be grand, Trish.' Rosie made herself comfortable in the middle seat of a row of three, with Mrs Blaney on her right and Kay Byrne on her left. Kay was in foils, and Mrs Blaney swathed in a towel-arranged turban style on her head.

'You were saying you'll have to do all your own housekeeping at the B&B yourself now, Mrs B?' Trish prompted.

'Oh, aye. That Katie is leaving Erin's Glen apparently,' Mrs Blaney confirmed. 'Leaving me in the lurch. Katie worked in the mornings at my guest house, had the afternoons off and then went to work in The Thatch in the evenings. That arrangement has worked well for years. But she felt the need to go now, despite the trouble it has created for me. I have a constant stream of guests – constant, even at this time of year. I don't know how I will keep up with it all.'

Trish tutted. 'Strange that after everything that's happened.' Trish looked around at the assembled group with a meaningful expression on her face. 'Strange that Katie has decided to leave now, after all these years?'

'Well, I'm not one to cast dispersions on anyone's character, but we all know what Katie was up to with that Sean. Rest in Peace.' Mrs Blaney paused and then continued piously, 'So we're best to leave it at that, Trish.' Mrs Blaney wagged a forefinger at the hairdresser and pursed her lips.

'Right, so, well said, Mrs B. Do any of you ladies want a top-up?' Trish nodded at the mugs and, taking one from Kay and snatching the other offered by Mrs Blaney, looked at Rosie. 'I'll get you your usual, love.' Trish disappeared behind a curtain to the mini-kitchen to prepare the drinks. The sound of mugs getting crashed about nearly drowned out the radio playing in the background.

Mrs Blaney piped up, 'Terrible business about Sean Flynn, isn't it?' Mrs Blaney looked around at her companions, waiting for a reaction, her pencilled eyebrows raised, emphasising the tone of expectation in her voice.

Rosie, usually so chatty, decided to sit this out and see what Kay or the others came up with. This visit to the hairdressers was proving to be particularly useful.

'It is indeed, Mrs Blaney.' Kay peered over her shoulder to check Trish was out of earshot.

When she thought Trish couldn't hear, she lowered her voice, 'I feel sorry for Trish. Imagine that happening just across the road. It must worry her, especially having a child in the house; I'd be distraught!'

Rosie was nodding in agreement.

'Ah, I wouldn't worry too much,' Trish's voice called out. She reappeared from the small kitchen, the clarity of her hearing astounding her three customers. 'To be honest, I think Sean had a skin-full, slipped over and died from hypothermia. I'd be shocked there was foul play.' With this reassuring opinion expressed, Trish passed around the mugs of steaming tea and began removing some foils from Kay's hair. 'Ah, we'll leave you to cook a bit longer,' Trish pronounced, continuing, 'We'll put you under the dryer; I'll just get the hood on you. Right, Rosie. Let's get you shampooed.' The sound of the gushing water and dryer over Kay halted any further conversation for the time being, and the assembled group were left to listen to the radio or pick up a magazine.

Mrs Blaney sat impatiently flicking through her *Woman's Weekly*, waiting for an opportunity to pursue the topic further. Her eyes moved between the magazine and Trish, watching as Trish washed

Rosie's hair. After a few minutes, Rosie emerged from the shampooing and was wrapped up in a towel.

Trish darted over to Kay. 'Let's get that dryer off and give you a few minutes to cool down.'

The noisy machine was silenced, and with relative quiet restored, Mrs Blaney put down her magazine and glanced at Trish. 'Your Seamus used to be pals with Sean, isn't that right?' Her arched eyebrows were raised even further.

'Mmm.' Trish was now behind Kay, pulling out the foils, a comb between her teeth, focused on examining Kay's tresses.

Mrs Blaney fixed her gaze on Trish. 'They had a falling out, didn't they?'

Rosie felt like she was at a tennis match, looking between Trish on one side and Mrs Blaney on the other.

'Ah, that was years ago, Mrs B.' Trish was dismissive and not keen to pursue the subject. 'Right, let's get you dried off, Mrs B.' Trish marched over and proceeded to remove the turban from Mrs Blaney's head, drying her hair with perhaps more vigour than was necessary, making further questions from this customer impossible.

When Mrs Blaney had recovered from the enthusiastic towel drying, she took a breath and prodded further, 'Oh right, for sure it was a long time ago, but I've often wondered about it.'

Trish ignored this further questioning and was focused on nimbly rolling Mrs Blaney's short hair onto rollers, with astonishing rapidity.

Mrs Blaney, obviously thinking Trish had not heard, repeated more loudly, 'I've often wondered what those boys would have fought about?'

Rosie sank slightly in her chair and pulled her *Ireland's Own* magazine over her face, thinking, 'The cheek of that woman!'

'Sure, there was no fight at all. Now, Mrs B, let's get you finished.' Trish was keen to shut down Mrs B's line of questioning and wheeled the drying hood over to her nosey client. The hairdresser was relieved to pull the hood down low over the older woman's head, switching the dryer on full blast – the mechanical whirring of the dryer silencing her at last.

Kay sat wide-eyed. Rosie caught her glance at her in the mirror and shook her head in tacit agreement to not pursue the 'Sean/Seamus' subject any further. However, it was difficult to ignore recent dramatic events completely.

Rosie turned the conversation to more positive outcomes. 'I'm glad to hear that Deirdre is making good progress in the hospital. Poor girl must have had such a shock, slipping into the river like that.'

Warming to the subject change, Trish answered, 'Oh aye, can you imagine it! She must have been freezing! She was lucky Mary Jo was out early that morning and found her; I dread to think what might have happened if she had been in that water any longer.'

The two other women shook their heads in agreement. Mrs Blaney, under the dryer, switched to its highest output, was watching their faces intently. She had done a course on lip reading and was now honing her skills.

Kay sighed sympathetically, empathising with the young woman who had been through so much recently. 'I think she was out looking for her cat. I know she was saying that he'd disappeared. She's attached to it, although I don't know why he keeps wandering off, but I suppose she was even more distraught with losing Sean…'

Now it was Rosie's turn to get her head scrubbed with a towel and her hair combed out. Trish moved around her, snipping and combing, keeping up the flow of conversation about Deirdre, 'Oh, she's such a timid wee thing. She never goes out, so that cat means the world to her. I hope he turns up when she leaves the hospital; she'll be glad of the company.'

'We'll all keep an eye out for him,' Rosie offered helpfully.

Trish glanced at Mrs Blaney, who was grimacing under the hood. Her face had reddened, and her arched eyebrows were now even closer to her hairline. There was a distinct scorching smell in the air. 'Trish, this is getting powerful hot under here,' she shouted above the noise, pointing up at the dryer hood.

Trish snapped the off switch on the hood. Mrs Blaney immediately jumped back, keen to get re-involved in the chat. Rosie looked at her, astounded by this woman's ability to steer the conversation. Her skill was of Olympic standard. If they gave out gold medals for nosiness, Mrs Blaney would be covered in them.

Just as Trish was pondering briefly on Mrs Blaney's skills, the older woman piped up again, 'Did I hear you talk about Deirdre?'

Kay smiled and nodded with just enough of a hint of positivity to give Mrs B the green light.

'Well, you know what I heard?' Mrs B leaned forward on her chair and turned to face her fellow customers. She waited a moment to add to the moment's tension, delighted to see the curious expressions on her companions' faces. Rosie and Kay looked agog. Although not fans of the nosey gossip, they were curious about the story concerning Deirdre.

Mrs B took a second more to revel in the attention and looked between the expectant faces. Her mouth, accentuated by the latest shade of pillar-box red lipstick, pursed. 'Well, the story goes that she was out looking for her cat.'

'We know that,' Trish snapped back.

Mrs B glanced at Trish and carried on almost without taking a breath, 'Well, I heard from Sarah-Jane, who works up at the hospital;

you know Sarah-Jane, her mother used to work for me at the guest house; Sarah Jane went to England to train to be a nurse but came back? She didn't like it over there. She never settled and had trouble with some neighbours...'

'Yes, yes, but what about Deirdre?' Rosie had abandoned her earlier resolve to stay silent. She could resist it no longer, was keen to discover what had happened, and was irritated by Mrs Blaney's side-tracking.

Mrs Blaney took a second to register her disdain for Rosie's impatience, her helmet of blue-grey curls shining now in the sunlight that slanted in through the shop's front window.

'Right, well, Sarah-Jane told me directly, first-hand, that she has been nursing Deirdre and that the police are involved now.' Mrs Blaney paused, enjoying her moment in the limelight.

The other women sat waiting for further illumination. Trish stood, brush in hand, looking blankly at Mrs Blaney.

'The police?' Rosie queried.

'Oh aye,' Mrs Blaney confirmed. 'Deirdre didn't fall. She was *pushed*.'

CHAPTER TWENTY-EIGHT

Fishing for Clues

Erin's Glen seemed to sigh a collective out-breath of relief as the weekend rolled around. This included Dan. It had been a tough week as one of the few trained officers in the town. Much of the hard graft of questioning, report writing and following up leads had been left to him. Resources were thin on the ground, and the local judicial will to find out what had happened to the unpopular Sean in his final minutes was half-hearted.

So, early on Saturday morning, Dan did what he usually did when he had a tough case to mull over: he went fishing. His wife packed up a 'piece' for him, a local word for a thick wedge of sandwiches to keep him fuelled up for a few hours on a cold bank. With his 'piece' and a flask of hot tea under his arm, Dan gathered up his fishing gear and proceeded down the road toward Abanculeen, close enough to walk.

The air was cold and still. The first ray of weak sunshine brought some warmth to his face and illuminated his ruddy features. The fresh air and promise of a good morning's fishing cheered him, and his usual bon vivre began to return. He found a suitable spot, shaded under some willow trees. The river was high but not running so fast this morning. Dan unfolded his green canvas chair to settle down for a bit of serious fishing. The dark, still pool of water reflected the overhanging tree and wispy white clouds above.

With his rod angled into the water, he had just got himself all setup when he spotted Ziggy. The curly-haired spaniel was bounding towards him, eyes sparkling and ears flapping, obviously making for him. Ziggy had rather too much enthusiasm for Dan's liking. A bit like his owner. Dan swore mildly under his breath. He liked dogs, but he was seeing a bit too much of Ziggy this week. As if he had read his mind, Ziggy came to a halt and looked Dan in the eye with an offended expression. He waited patiently until Rosie caught up with him, looking like the epitome of canine obedience.

'We're just out for a wee run, Dan; hope we haven't bothered you.' Rosie didn't wait for an answer. 'It's a lovely soft morning,' she offered cheerfully.

'Aye,' Dan answered drily, knowing what was coming next. He kept his eyes fixed ahead.

'We've had quite a week in Erin's Glen.'

'We have for sure.'

'What do you make of it, Dan?'

Abandoning all hope of a quiet few minutes to himself, Dan slowly put the rod to one side on the ground and turned to face Rosie.

'Well, we've got one body that no one with any authority seems interested in investigating and a near miss with Deirdre. I feel so bad about what might have happened; I'm loath to try questioning the poor girl again.'

Rosie knew when to be quiet, and she waited patiently until Dan took a few minutes to reflect on his regret about Deirdre. She kept her gaze fixed on the policeman, not wanting to risk missing any nuances of expression. She remained silent as he paused and continued, 'The truth is I don't know her intentions or what happened; all I know is I ask the girl questions, and she turns up in the river the next day. What do you think?'

Rosie agreed it didn't reflect well on Dan's professional diplomacy or tact. Nevertheless, she tried to reassure him.

'Well, sure, you were just doing your job, and as you say, we don't know what the story is there. But thank God she seems to be recovering well, from what I've heard. She's struck up a friendship with Marie, and I believe she's been to see her, so at least Deirdre has plenty of friends around her. No one blames you, Dan. You're too hard on yourself.'

'Aye, well, I don't feel like I'm doing the job very well. I'm no closer to finding out what happened to Sean.'

The conversation was now going in the direction Rosie wanted. Keen for any scent of a clue, she encouraged Dan to continue.

'So, what have we got then, Dan?' Rosie folded her arms and put her head to one side. She frowned in concentration as she listened to his answer.

He looked slightly askance at the amateur sleuth, but he was grateful for anyone who would listen; he carried on. 'Well, the pathologist faxed through his report last night. Sean died sometime between 10 pm and the early hours of Thursday morning. He was the victim of a blow to the head with a blunt object. I was first on the scene, and no footprints or weapons were visible. After Sean left Shenanigans, no one saw him. The heavy snowfall kept everyone indoors and concealed the body until I found him the next morning.'

This was pretty much as Rosie understood the situation, but she was grateful for confirmation regarding the cause of death.

'So, someone bludgeoned Sean on the back of the head?'

'That's about right,' Dan agreed as he lifted his rod and inspected what was on the hook.

'Where was Jim Noonan?' Rosie queried.

'His got an alibi. He was out at a trade fair in Rocksheelan. He stayed over at the hotel there. He has multiple witnesses and we spoke to him on the phone while he was still there.'

Rosie looked thoughtful. 'It's just as well Jim has an alibi; otherwise, it wouldn't look good for him, would it?' Rosie queried.

'Aye, right enough,' Dan confirmed.

She brought to mind the scene from Thursday morning. With her photographic memory, she did not need to peruse police pictures.

'Right outside The Thatch,' she murmured to herself. A theory was forming in her mind, but it was too ridiculous to share with the seasoned policeman, so she kept it to herself. She needed more evidence to substantiate what she thought might have happened.

Dan stared dully ahead. He sat slumped on his fishing stool. Rosie was just about to bid him farewell when he started to rock on the lightweight canvas seat. Something had bitten the tasty morsel on the end of his rod. Dan got control of the wavering rod and reeled in the prize. It was a silvery trout, a shiny beauty that would undoubtedly be baked with a bit of lemon and parsley that night.

'Well, I wish reeling in whoever killed poor Sean was as easy!' Dan cast Rosie a happier look, and with that, she trotted off along the riverbank with Ziggy at her heels, determined now to add substance to prove the theory she was, for now, keeping to herself. The early sunshine had disappeared behind a bank of grey clouds, and an icy wind drove Ziggy and Rosie back to the warmth of her bungalow.

Chapter Twenty-Nine

Home is Where the Heart Is

The previous evening, after Trish and Roisin had left the shop, Marie had gone through her usual routine of locking up, but this time, she locked the shop door from the outside and carried on along Rainbow Row. The brightly painted fronts of the buildings glowed eerily in the streetlights, the colours distorted by the yellow hue of the artificial light. True to her word, Marie was on her way to the cottage hospital to visit Deirdre. Mary Jo had prompted her but was grateful for the nun's gentle urging. Marie had been drawn to Deirdre, and although they were superficially quite different, she felt they had much in common. A sharp frost was beginning to settle, and the pavement was starting to glisten with a silvery, wet sheen as Marie made her way along.

On impulse, Marie stepped into the office of Erin Cabs, the local taxi company. She hadn't bought a car yet, and it was a bit too far to walk or cycle to the hospital, especially on such a cold, bleak night. Marie snuggled into her scarf and realised that her short biker jacket was probably inadequate for the freezing conditions.

'Evening, Marie.' A woman with an unnaturally black perm tamed by a colourful headscarf sat behind a desk. Marie was slightly taken aback that the woman knew her name. 'I'm Maureen. Call me psychic, but I reckon you're looking for a taxi.' Maureen's face creased into a hearty laugh at her own joke. Marie nodded, still a little non-plussed by the extroverted taxi operator. 'Where are you going, love?' Maureen enquired.

'The hospital.'

Marie saw a look of concern pass over Maureen's face; the taxi operator seemed to think Marie might need some immediate hospital attention. Noticing her expression, Marie added, 'Oh, not for me, don't worry, it's not an emergency. I'm going to visit my friend.'

'Ah, that would be that wee Deirdre, then?'

Marie was surprised by this woman's depth of knowledge about her business, but accepting that this was the reality of living in a small town, she just shrugged, smiled, and nodded, 'Yes, that's right. I am popping over there to see how she's doing – Mary Jo asked me.' Maureen had a slightly disturbing way of looking directly into Marie's eyes, nodding, and waiting for more information.

'Terrible business, all that,' Maureen tutted and paused. Then, seeing that Marie was not about to offer any more information, she pressed a button on the machine on the desk and shouted, 'Maniac, I've got Marie here wanting a ride to the hospital.'

Marie was a little alarmed at the name of her driver, and just as she was about to query it, a smiling, rosy-cheeked middle-aged man of gigantic proportions bounded into the taxicab office. He was clothed in a brown leather jacket that looked like it was straining across his broad shoulders. He rubbed his hands together in an effort to warm them. 'Good evening, ladies. I've just come back from the bus station in Rocksheelan.'

Maureen nodded, 'Righto, so that's Katie away then.' Maureen looked at the taxi driver with raised eyebrows, waiting for confirmation. He nodded and turned to his latest passenger. 'Marie, your chariot awaits.' The cheerful driver gestured towards the taxi parked outside, still running its engine.

'Bye.' The taxi operator waved and winked. Marie turned towards the door, not quite sure what to expect of the jolly giant who was her driver. He stood by the open passenger door as Marie slid in.

'I'm Jakob Manieck, but all my friends call me Manieck.' He turned to grin at Marie, who had felt slightly disturbed about being driven by a 'maniac'. As if reading her mind, he reassured her, 'Don't worry, the locals mispronounce my name. It's their little joke! I drive well.' Jakob Manieck pronounced his name with a slight Eastern European accent that puzzled Marie. She was about to ask him about this when she spotted some Rosary beads hanging from the rearview mirror. She wasn't sure whether to be concerned or comforted by their presence.

'What brought you to Erin's Glen?' Marie asked.

'My heart!'

Marie looked confused.

Manieck explained, 'My family came to the north of Ireland after the invasion of Poland in 1939. I was a small boy when we arrived and grew up in Newry. In time, I met my beautiful Irish Colleen from Erin's Glen and followed my heart. So here I am!' Manieck put a hand to his chest and sighed dramatically. Marie couldn't help but be charmed by Jacob Manieck's warmth.

'How lovely! Who is she?' Her own curiosity surprised her, but the local social conventions were seemingly rubbing off on her.

Manieck gave a little giggle. 'She's literally a Colleen! Her name is Colleen!'

'Ah, I see! Of course, she runs the delicatessen shop Colleen's Cuts!' Marie joined in the laughter.

'We married in Erin's Glen. It was a wonderful day. My mother and father and all my Irish friends were there. Sadly, my cousins from Poland couldn't attend, but it was so beautiful.'

Manieck looked at Marie in the rearview mirror to emphasise his depth of emotion, his eyes glistening with tears as he recalled his special day many years before.

Manieck kept up a conversation about his family, friends, and previous jobs.

'I used to be a builder, but now I have a bad back,' Manieck grimaced in the mirror. 'All I can do is drive and help out at the shop. Here we are.' Manieck pulled up smoothly outside the small semicircular building that housed the local cottage hospital. 'I will wait for you and take you home when you are ready. Don't worry, I'm not busy. Erin's Glen is a quiet gig!' Manieck broke into more laughter as he came around to open her door and waved her off as she produced her purse. 'Later, no rush.' He made a brushing-away gesture and shook his head.

Marie strode into the small hospital and checked in at the front desk. A short nurse with a blonde bob accompanied her down through a quiet ward.

'Deirdre, visitor for you.' She pulled a curtain back and revealed a pale, dazed-looking Deirdre sitting in the bed. Deirdre immediately smiled when she saw Marie. Seeing her petite figure clothed in a standard-issue hospital gown made Marie's heart lurch. She felt for this girl who seemed lonely and a little lost.

'Oh God, love ya.' Deirdre looked appreciatively at the items Marie produced from her bag: a Tupperware box of rock buns, some wool and knitting needles, and a copy of *U Magazine*. 'You're a star.' She smiled, smoothing her hand over the magazine and glancing at the dark brown buns in the opaque plastic box as if they were luxury items.

'I'm afraid I was a bit distracted today. These are not my best.' Marie was a little embarrassed by the slightly blackened efforts she was offering. 'They are true to their name anyway. Hopefully, they won't break your teeth!'

'Ach, no worries, you're so talented with your artistic displays and running a business; for goodness' sake, you can't be doing everything.' After a pause, Deirdre continued, 'I suppose I'm the hot topic in Erin's Glen then.' Deirdre didn't look happy about the prospect.

'I won't lie, Deirdre, you know better than me what it's like, but I'm sure people are just worried about you.'

'Aye, and embarrassed, a lot of them couldn't look me straight in the eyes after Sean was found dead.' A look of anger flashed across Deirdre's face and added a shrill tone to her words.

Marie remained silent. She sensed much resentment seethed below Deirdre's mild exterior and that she needed to talk.

'It's been awful, Marie. I hate being the centre of attention at the best of times, and all those oul biddies are only too keen to share their opinion on what's happened to him. The other day, I overheard Mrs Blaney talking about me in the post office, analysing my every move and expression. It was like she thought I'd done him in myself. I only caught the tail end of the conversation when I went in. It was awful.' Deirdre sighed. 'Anyway, thanks for coming in, Marie. It's lovely to have company with no pressure. I'm tired of people putting their nose into my business.'

The truth was, Marie *was* curious to know more about what had happened but was polite enough to make small talk and be patient. Deirdre would open up when she was ready. Deirdre herself had a knack for getting Marie to talk about her background, and before she knew it, Marie was sharing the story that had brought her to Erin's Glen.

'Don't worry, I'll keep it to myself,' Deirdre reassured Marie and leaned over to pat her hand. 'I've had my disappointments in life too.' The young woman sighed, seeming older than her years. 'Sure, who hasn't,' she continued.

Marie was struck by the wearied way Deirdre talked about her life. She found out a little more about Deirdre's family and the losses she had in recent years. Tears welled up in Marie's eyes in empathy for all the sad experiences that Deirdre had gone through.

'So, I ended up with Sean. I know he was carrying on behind my back.' Deirdre gave a hollow little laugh. 'God forgive me, but I don't miss him. That's terrible, isn't it?' Deirdre looked at Marie.

'No, it's not terrible, Deirdre; he behaved shabbily towards you and took advantage of your situation.' This time, Marie reached out to her friend, with her pale hair fanned out on the pillows behind her. 'You need to concentrate on yourself now and on getting well.'

'You know what has really wound me up in all of this?' Deirdre shifted herself in bed, energised by the anger she felt about recent events. 'That Dan, coming round to my place. It felt like he was making out I'd clobbered Sean myself. I was fuming, I can tell you!'

Marie saw some of the strength of Deirdre's spirit in that moment – the grit of her character that had kept her going through some difficult days. Marie had wondered if Deirdre perhaps *had* felt overwhelmed by grief or hopelessness after Sean's death and had, in fact, jumped into the river in desperation. But now, seeing the spark in her friend's eye, she doubted it. Marie could relate to Deirdre; people assumed that because they were mild-mannered and quiet, they were a walkover, but Deirdre was obviously made of sterner stuff than some of the locals might have thought.

'I chucked Dan out!' Deirdre declared. Marie looked at her fragile-looking friend and smiled. The image of this diminutive girl throwing the burly police officer out of her house amused Marie. Deirdre caught her friend's eye, and as if reading her mind, she giggled. 'You should have seen the look of shock on his face! He couldn't believe wee me, all meek and mild would push him out of the door!' At this, Deirdre started to howl with laughter.

Nurse Blonde Bob looked up from her nurse's station with a frown and a finger to her lips. 'Shush!' she scolded them. Despite shaking her head vigorously, her solid hairdo didn't move.

Marie and Deirdre gave her a cursory nod but continued to giggle, stifling their sniggers as best they could, their shoulders shaking and eyes streaming. After a few minutes and a few deep breaths, they composed themselves.

Marie almost forgot about the sad circumstances of the last few days and felt relaxed and happy in the company of her troubled friend.

Deirdre continued, 'I'll have a word with that Dan when I get out of here about that morning I ended up in the water. I was walking along the river looking for Patch, he goes down to look at the fish there and—'

A short bell rang, indicating the visiting time was up.

'...Marie, I felt someone give me a shove in the back.'

Marie reeled back in shock. 'Are you sure?'

'As sure as sugar. Someone was trying to push me in. I'm sure of it. I'll be getting on to Dan tomorrow. Never mind him giving *me* the third degree!'

'But who?' Marie queried. 'Who would do that to you?'

Nurse Blonde Bob was marching towards the bed now with a threatening look on her face, 'Visiting time is over, ladies.' She looked disapprovingly at Marie, obviously her biker jacket, heavy boots, and long trailing knitted scarf not a style she appreciated. Marie looked back at Deirdre. On impulse, she moved back towards her, kissed her forehead, and squeezed her hand. 'I'll be back tomorrow evening.'

She caught the eye of the sturdy nurse, her hands on her hips, looking between the two young women.

'*Miss!*' Nurse Blonde Bob was losing patience.

Getting the message, Marie wound her scarf around her neck and pulled on a woolly hat, bracing herself for the cold air outside. For a split second, Marie was tempted to salute the bossy nurse and click her heels, but Marie resisted her childish urge and instead smiled sweetly and walked towards the exit. As she approached the glass doors to leave the building, she could see Maniek spring out of the driver's seat and wave, his chubby face slightly reddened by the heat of the car engine. A few tufts of blonde hair sprouted from under his black knitted hat.

'Miss,' he said more warmly than the nurse. 'Let's get you home.'

Marie liked the sound of that... 'Home.'

However, despite Marie's warm feelings about her new place of abode, it was deeply unnerving to think a killer was on the loose. Just who had pushed Deirdre into the river?

Chapter Thirty

Pooling Ideas

The same evening as Marie's hospital visit, Mary Jo and Rosie had also shared a companionable meeting. They were enjoying a cosy tea at the end of their working week. Mary Jo sat back in a comfortable, winged armchair with a floral pattern, mug of tea in hand and plate of goodies on her lap; she considered what they knew. Both women were tired from their exertions this week, and the warm fire, baked goods and soothing warm drinks lulled them into a relaxed state. Mary Jo looked thoughtfully into the fire, turning recent events over in her mind. More agitated than her companion, Rosie munched quickly on the baked goods and took gulps of tea, her thoughts darting all over the place.

At last, Mary Jo gave in with a sigh, 'It's no good, Rosie, we'll have to sleep on this one. Let's have a break and see what rises to the surface.' Mary Jo tapped the side of her head and nodded sagely.

Due to the lack of information and inspiration, Rosie and Mary Jo had agreed to reconvene later on Sunday. They both resolved to find out more. Mary Jo was often out and about shopping, walking, or running in the town and would no doubt get to talk to someone who could shine a bit more light on recent events. Rosie, too, was sure she could unearth some more information. Indeed, after her chance meeting with Dan, Rosie felt that more of a firm idea of what might have happened to Sean was forming in her mind. It might sound far-fetched even to the open-minded Mary Jo, so Rosie continued to turn this theory over privately in her thoughts for a while longer.

This time, Rosie went up to Riverside House to visit her friend. The nuns were always pleased to have a visitor. Rosie reckoned they looked forward more to welcoming Ziggy and his entertaining antics, but Rosie didn't mind being upstaged by her endearing spaniel. Rosie was accepted into the sitting room of Riverside House and made welcome; after a few pleasantries, Sister Angela took Ziggy off to the kitchen for a tasty treat, and Mary Jo and Rosie got down to discussing the matters in hand.

The two women shared ideas and theories. Many of their ruminations were based on piecing together snatches of gossip garnered during the week. Mary Jo was the first to share a theory. 'You know who I got talking to on Thursday evening?'

'Who?' Rosie queried through a mouthful of Blackberry Crumble tray bake.

'Mrs Carroll.'

'Oh aye, I know her; her girl, Liz, plays the accordion?'

'The very same,' Mary Jo confirmed. 'Anyway, she told me that Gerry's girlfriend has returned to Dublin.'

Rosie looked a bit blank.

'You know that lovely girl, Finula?'

'Right...' Rosie nodded thoughtfully. 'And?'

'Well, that struck me as odd.' Mary Jo waited for Rosie's response.

After absorbing this news, Rosie clarified Mary Jo's thinking. 'So, you believe Finula or Gerry have something to do with Sean's murder?'

'Maybe.' Mary Jo shrugged.

'Mmm,' Rosie chewed more of her crumble and considered this line of thought. 'No, I'm not convinced. I'm sure it has something to do with old Will.' Rosie waggled her dessert fork at Mary Jo as she spoke, emphasising her line of thought.

Mary Jo looked at Rosie blankly. She then blinked her bright blue eyes and repeated, 'Will. You think *Will* killed Sean?' Mary Jo looked doubtful. 'Sure, he's not even here; by all accounts, he's gone wherever the good Lord has sent him.' Mary Jo blessed herself as she considered Will's possible eternal home.

Rosie went on undeterred. 'Well, there was all that underhand shady business with burning the car showroom and workshop. Will is Jim Noonan's cousin, and I reckon they were in communication.' Rosie finished with an affirmative nod of her head.

'How do you know?' pressed Mary Jo, her eyes narrowed.

At this, Rosie sighed. Specific images flashed into her mind, but she found it hard to match them to exact times, locations, and circumstances. That was the problem with her memory. She could remember images precisely, but the surrounding facts were distorted. This was especially true when the photos themselves seemed unimportant or mundane at the time.

'I'm not sure how I know, Mary Jo. But I'm determined to find out. And find out I will. I will inveigle myself into The Thatch and discover what's happening there.'

Mary Jo was not convinced but had been impressed by the results of Rosie's photographic memory in the past. She was sure she just needed time and further prompting for the facts to fall into place.

Mary Jo had made notes in a coded form and retrieved her spiral-bound notebook to go through her jottings. 'Point number one, S.F. Who? Right, well, we've discussed that for now. Let's move on to point number two, F.G. and Miss M – who? I've just written this in coded form with the initials to conceal identity,' Mary Jo confirmed, pencil to her lips and a look of deep concentration on her face.

Rosie looked at her friend slightly askance; she got the point and didn't need Mary Jo to get all officious. Mary Jo ignored the look and continued, 'Well, there are these letters; we know Father Gerard and Miss McGrath both received letters. They haven't stopped since Sean died. As we now know, both continue to receive them.'

Rosie nodded. Father Gerard had confided in her up to a point, and she knew that the threats had, in fact, been stepped up. She was aware Miss McGrath had spoken to Mary Jo in more detail. Mary Jo had confided in Rosie and told her that the letters said the secret would be exposed unless a large sum of money was handed over – the point for collecting the illicit package being a phone box at the foot of Slieve Cairn. No time or date had yet been set for collecting the money. The messages continued to consist of characters cut crudely from newspapers and hand-delivered. As yet, neither the priest nor the head teacher had informed the police. This was partly due to other more pressing matters that week and partly due to the embarrassment of the profoundly personal issue the blackmail alluded to. It was apparent that neither the priest nor the school principal wanted to be placed under public scrutiny.

'Why pick on Miss McGrath and Father Gerard?' Mary Jo tapped her pencil against her teeth.

Rosie and Mary Jo considered what characteristics the two notable figures in the town shared. The head teacher and the priest were prominent figures in Erin's Glen; both could be described as pillars of the community. What else did they have in common?

Both had known each other from childhood; there was only a few years' difference in age, Miss McGrath being the younger of the pair.

As Mary Jo travelled back in her memory, she hit on the very same thought Rosie had in mind then. A memory from all those decades ago that was to have more bearing on recent events than anyone might have considered before now. Rosie was unsure how much Miss McGrath had confided in the nun. She was reluctant to break a confidence shared with her by Father Gerard and was relieved to see her quick-witted friend join the dots of this puzzle.

A light of recognition came on in Mary Jo's eyes. She paused and blinked, and looked at Rosie.

'Are you thinking what I'm thinking?'

Rosie nodded.

So taken were they by this latest epiphany that both women forgot momentarily about point three on Mary Jo's notes: who had pushed Deirdre into the river?

However, that question would have to wait. Deirdre was recovering well and would be discharged in time for Sean's funeral. Erin's Glen braced itself for this final send-off for this young man who was contentious in life – and death.

Chapter Thirty-One

An IT Revolution

Monday morning soon rolled around; Rosie had been dreading this day. She had avoided previous invitations and suggestions for dates, but it could be put off no longer – IT training day.

A perceptive officer, Pauline, at the training centre for the Diocese, had sensed Rosie's reluctance to join any of the groups of church secretaries from the locality. After numerous attempts to get Rosie signed up, Pauline phoned and promised her a one-to-one session with Rajan, who had worked magic with the other ladies lacking confidence in IT. Pauline had organised for Rajan to come straight to the office at St Brigid's and show Rosie how to operate the machine Rosie had kept shrouded in the corner.

Ziggy had accompanied her to work that day. 'Moral support,' she had informed him before he gleefully jumped into the Mini to travel with her to the office.

Rajan was due to arrive at 10 am, and right on time, she saw an unfamiliar van pull into the church car park.

'This'll be him,' Rosie informed Ziggy, already up and out of his basket, ready to greet the visitor. Rosie opened the door with Ziggy at her heels before Rajan could ring the bell.

'Good morning! Mrs O'Reilly?' Rajan beamed at her enquiringly. Rosie felt entirely overcome by the brightness of his smile and the sparkle in his eyes. His whole face seemed to emit a glow that immediately entranced the parish secretary.

'Come in, come in! You'll be wanting some tea after your journey.' Rosie already had the tea brewing in the rotund pot encased in a handknitted cosy to keep the contents warm.

'Wonderful tea-cosy! I love it!' Rajan enthused, admiring the nativity scene depicted on the front, complete with a knitted angel at the top.

'My mother knitted it,' Rosie informed him, delighted that a man of such good taste was in her presence.

Rajan settled down opposite Rosie and sipped his tea. Much to her relief, he was seemingly in no rush to talk about computers.

'And who's this?' Rajan bent down and gave Ziggy a tickle under the chin. Ziggy looked approvingly at Rajan and was further enamoured when the IT instructor shared his scone with his new canine friend.

After some chit-chat about Rajan's pet dachshund, Taj, Rajan brushed the crumbs from his hands and dabbed at his mouth with a napkin. 'So, this is the machine in question?' Rajan nodded at the dark shape in the corner.

Rosie, tight-lipped, replied without enthusiasm, 'That's the one.'

Rajan sprung out of his chair and bounded across the office. He pulled off the grey-coloured cover with a flourish and revealed the boxy monitor, computer tower and a coil of cables. Rosie swallowed, sensing an unfamiliar wave of anxiety flood over her.

'Right. Let's get this beast tamed.' Rajan pulled cables out of the snaky tangle and deftly plugged them into the back of the tower and monitor.

'Okay, Rosie, you don't need to worry about all this process.' Rajan waved his hands over the cables with a flourish. He had noticed her nervous gaze as he performed his magic with the wires. 'That's my job. Your first job will be to get this beauty fired up.' He waited a second to make sure she was giving him her full attention. She was, in fact, captivated by her colourful instructor. Duly reassured of her attention, he carried on, 'So, you press this button to get her going.' Rajan indicated a button at the front, pointing at it with a beautifully manicured forefinger. He waited a second, 'Go on, Rosie, you do it.' He sat patiently while she took a breath and waggled her finger towards the button. Gingerly, Rosie pressed it, gulping back her anxiety. The screen flickered and emitted a blue light. Rosie blinked in surprise.

Rajan clapped his hands together in delight. 'Ah, fantastic! You are a goddess, bringing the dead to life!' He smiled at Rosie as if she genuinely had performed a miracle. Ziggy popped up from his basket in alarm, but realising all was well, he settled back down, ears twitching. Rosie's earlier hesitance was beginning to subside; she gave a shy grin, pleased with her evident progress.

As Rajan explained the mysteries of the mouse, the cursor, icons and screens, Rosie felt like she was learning a new language. She was a bit confused to see that a floppy disc was, in fact, a very firm-looking square thing but accepted Rajan's explanation of its incongruent name.

Rosie's almost continuous refrain was, 'Well, I never knew that!' A ray of sunshine slanted into the office as if on cue, illuminating their faces. The sun's rays enhanced the sheen of Rajan's bright lavender-coloured silk shirt. The spring light glinted off the gold jewellery that adorned his neck, fingers, and wrists. Rosie could hardly concentrate on what he was saying, distracted as she was by his flamboyant style of dress and accessories.

The training session ended after two hours of explanation, demonstration, and effusive praise. Rosie blushed as Rajan exclaimed, 'You temptress!' responding to her offer of more tea and scones. Rajan regretfully informed her that he needed to get off for his next appointment with Mrs Doyle at St Brendan's. Rosie knew Mrs Doyle and she sniffed, 'Good luck with that one!' feeling suddenly all superior. Rosie knew Mrs Doyle couldn't even work the electric typewriter.

'You have been a delight to meet, Miss O'Reilly.' Rajan took her hand briefly, and for a second, she thought he was going to kiss it, but a little to her disappointment, he squeezed it gently and gave her hand a little shake. He looked into her eyes, 'You keep up the good work, Miss O'Reilly; never have I worked with a lady who picked up the basics so quickly, your fingers fly across that keyboard like butterflies in flight. No need to be worried about lack of skill; it's all there.' Rajan tapped the side of his temple lightly. Rosie coyly smiled, looking sideways at Ziggy, who was raising an eyebrow and looking slightly askance at the tall, colourful character seeming to fill the small office.

'In years to come, all these dusty old books will be replaced. Your record keeping will be revolutionised!' Rajan swept his lean arm expansively in the direction of the shelf of leatherbound books, decades of parish records above the desk. This reminded Rosie of a small matter she must check later. She made a mental note to check on something that had been niggling her earlier.

Rosie watched Rajan swiftly but carefully pack his bag, wrapping cables and placing items back into their intended compartments. With a flourish, he swirled his dark blue jacket around his shoulders and strode towards the front door, suddenly stopping before opening it.

'Before I go, I have a gift for you.' He put his hand into a pocket at the front of his bag and produced a flat item wrapped in clear plastic.

Rosie looked at it curiously. The thin rectangle depicted Mary with the baby Jesus in a Greek one-dimensional style. She looked at him with curiosity.

'A mouse mat with a picture to help you tell the difference between your icons and your icons! Sorry, my little joke for the secretaries of the parish!' Rajan shrugged his shoulders and laughed.

Rosie smiled indulgently. 'Oh, you! You're a case!' she giggled.

'So, I shall venture forth to spread the good news of the IT revolution. Go well, my lady, and enjoy your beautiful machine's convenience, speed, and efficiency.' And with that, Rosie watched Rajan's tall figure stride across the car park back to his van.

Rosie returned to her small office and glanced at the leather-bound parish records on the shelf. Rajan's reference to the old tombs had reminded her of something she had meant to look up earlier. With Ziggy looking at her, she climbed up on the small step stool and retrieved the book she was looking for – Baptism Records 1950–1955. She ran her finger down the entries from 1950. Familiar surnames kept appearing with some regularity – Blaney, Coffey, Cushnahan, Dunleavy, Flynn, Foyle, Gallaher, Kennedy, Lehane, Mac Auley, McGrath, Molloy, Neary, O'Hagan, O'Hara, O'Mally, O'Reilly, Quinn, Rooney – but one name stood out.

'That's the one!' Rosie jabbed at an entry in the record with satisfied recognition. Her memory was propelled into gear, and everything started to fall into place. Rosie thought it had been a grand day as a contented smile spread across her face.

'Right, Ziggy, that's us. Let's go.'

Chapter Thirty-Two

Valedictions and Accusations

A few days later, in the same parish office, Father Gerard struggled to write a homily for Sean's funeral. In Erin's Glen, funerals usually took place within a few days of the person's passing. So, Sean's send-off had been long delayed due to the demands of the pathologist and the coroner. Father Gerard, a soft-hearted man himself, felt for the poor Deirdre; despite other people's opinions about Sean, he was sure she would miss him terribly.

He was relieved that the various professionals and authorities seemed to have satisfied themselves as regards the cause of death; it was clear it was foul play, not an accidental death as some had thought – or hoped. Gerard himself had indeed hoped and prayed that Sean's death was somehow just an unfortunate accident brought on by too much drink and freezing weather. Still, the professionals confirmed it was indeed a nasty and deliberate blow to the head that had been the cause of death. However, *who* was responsible for inflicting Sean's premature demise was still open to question.

Father Gerard had become accustomed to speaking at funerals of deceased marginal members of his parish. Many people had little to do with the church regularly. The priest was sadly only too aware of the falling numbers of parishioners at Mass each week. People only seemed interested in attending church for the rites of passage of baptism, marriage, and death. He had seen little of some people in between these life events. He considered this fact ruefully and tried to drag his attention back to the matter, writing a few well-considered words about this young man he only knew from a distance.

He sighed and tried to think hard of kind words to say about Sean that would avoid the banality these situations could descend into. As the priest tried to focus his mind, he couldn't help his thoughts drifting back to recent, more personal events.

Miss McGrath had been to see him. She had appeared rather dramatically at the back of the church when he had been kneeling at prayer one afternoon recently. She was an old friend. Many years before, their friendship had blossomed into a brief romance. Of course, they were only teenagers then, long before he had gone off to the seminary to train to be a priest. When he told Mairead, the name he always used when he thought of Miss McGrath, that he was considering going to the seminary to train to be a priest, Mairead had backed off. At the time, he knew she was hurt and upset, but she had respected his decision and never tried to rekindle any romance or even a close personal friendship with him. He tried to recall all the details, but it was decades ago. They were both not much more than children themselves.

But that's what Mairead had been to see him about. She confided in him that she had been getting horrible letters about 'their secret'.

Father Gerard had brushed off his worry about the author of the letters. After all, there was no real scandal concerning the romance he and Mairead had shared all those years before, was there?

Miss McGrath had sat next to him on the pew in the church and been categorical. 'Ignore them, Gerard. Whoever is writing them will get bored and move on to someone else. Goodness knows there's probably plenty of sinners in Erin's Glen who have secrets to hide.'

Father Gerard tended to agree. As a priest, he was privy to all sorts of information on his flock's shady dealings and misdeeds.

However, he still felt unsettled. Accusations concerning his personal life were one thing, but blackmail was something else entirely.

Despite these personal ruminations, Father Gerard managed to pen a few words about this misunderstood young man whose send-off he would be officiating. In truth, he would be relieved when it was all over. There had been some unpleasantness about who was paying for the funeral. Will, Sean's father, was presumed dead, and Sean's mother had passed away when Sean was a little boy. The financial burden fell on the publican, Jim, who was less than pleased.

'What a sorry state of affairs.' Father Gerard sighed and put the finishing touches to his homily to be shared at Sean's funeral.

The day of the funeral was clear and bright. A few brave daffodils danced about in the breeze in the churchyard, thus reminding the inhabitants of Erin's Glen that spring was in the air despite the heaviness of their hearts.

Inside the church, some weak sunshine illuminated the richly coloured stained glass windows, casting beautiful, multicoloured projections onto the church's marble floor. A heavy pall of intense smoke was in the air, desirable to the olfactory senses and the eye. Whorls of incense appeared in the sun's rays that slanted through the windows.

There was a calm and respectful silence in the church. A few coughs and whispers here and there.

Sean's remains were in the closed coffin at the front of the church. It was draped in an orange, white and green tricolour flag and strewn with shamrocks. Although the local community did not understand Sean well, they knew he was a proud Irishman. The national flag and little green symbol of Ireland would have been to his liking.

The gathering was a small one by Erin's Glen standards. A few of the funeral-attending faithful from the parish were there – a small group of older adults who attended every funeral whether they knew the person well or not. There were representatives from the local community in the form of teaching staff from the girls' school where Deirdre worked and a few shopkeepers known to Sean. Neither of the local publicans was present, despite Sean having spent so much of his life in their company.

Deirdre was present, looking frail but determined to say goodbye to this young man she believed she understood better than anyone else. Marie flanked her on one side and Miss Byrne from the school on the other. People in the congregation glanced around, uncomfortably aware that Sean's closest blood relative, Jim Noonan, was not yet present. As they looked towards the back of the church, they would have seen that Miss McGrath had slipped in the back with Mary Jo. The two women had managed to get away from school. Deirdre looked back and gave them a small smile and a nod. She appreciated the kindness of these two older ladies who were there to support her and show their respects to the young man with whom she had shared a home.

Outside the church door, a few local lads were smoking and chatting quietly in the gentle sunshine. They had known Sean from school, and a few had drunk with him. Not being frequent church attendees, they had decided to keep a distance from the religious send-off; they would all go for a jar afterwards to say their goodbyes.

Unusually for Erin's Glen, no wake had been organised. Sean spent his last night before his send-off in the church. The community had assumed Jim Noonan would arrange a boozy get-together around the coffin, but no such event had been organised. All concluded it was a strange ending to a strange tale.

A peaceful quiet descended on the church as the organ started to crank out the first hymn. Father Gerard appeared from the vestry in full church vestments and approached the altar, walking slowly and solemnly. He genuflected in front of the altar and turned to face the congregation. He went to raise his right hand to make the sign of the cross when—

'You oul hypocrite!'

The congregation, as a whole, gasped and turned to face the owner of the voice, silhouetted as it was in the doorway, the sunshine blinding their eyes.

A slurred, gravelly voice thundered up from the back of the church. Father Gerard stood in suspended animation, his hand in mid-air.

'And you, you oul witch, pretend to be all prim and proper! I know about you! You and him and your dirty little secret... I know.' At this, an arm was flung out expansively toward Miss McGrath. Rather too energetically for the figure, despite its width, it became unbalanced and toppled over.

The congregation now turned in unison to face the front. Father Gerard met his parish and gave the most honest speech he had ever made.

Chapter Thirty-Three

Time for Truth

'You're a disgrace!' Rosie scolded Jim as he stumbled back into the priest's house next door to the church. After Jim's outburst in the church, Rosie helped him out and into the presbytery with the help of some of the lads by the doorway. Jim lurched into the kitchen and dropped his heavy frame onto a kitchen chair by the large pine table. Rosie had commanded Jim to drink a cup of black coffee, which she was told had a sobering effect. Vile black tar, she thought as she handed him the mug. Ziggy had been waiting in the kitchen, he now marched up and down the room, taking his lead from Rosie. All the while, giving Jim disapproving glances as the unsteady man slurped coffee from his mug.

After a few gulps of the sobering brew, Jim could stagger precariously out to Rosie's little car. Getting the large, lumbering lump of a man into the back of her Mini would be impossible, so she shoved him in the front seat, and Ziggy jumped in the back.

As Rosie drove along the road back to The Thatch, Dan passed by on his bicycle. Dan had not been present in the church and had decided to circulate the town to keep an eye on things. He waved and looked slightly perplexed at the strange trio, Rosie looking ahead bedraggled with her wispy grey hair, glasses askew, Jim Noonan slumped asleep in the passenger seat, and Ziggy sat on the back seat behind the two humans, his furry face thrust over Jim's shoulder. Dan watched as the car passed, probably a bit too fast, but Dan dismissed this detail, realising Rosie was perhaps on a mission.

The Mini screeched to a juddering halt outside Jim's bar. Jim was jolted awake; he opened the car door and almost fell out of the passenger seat onto the pavement. He righted himself slowly and, with a rolling gait, approached his premises and pushed through the front doors. After hesitating, he made his way into the bar's lounge area. By then, he had sobered up a little but was barely coherent. Appearing exhausted, he threw himself on one of the red velvet lounge banquette seats and promptly fell asleep. Rosie and Ziggy had followed him in from the car, and both watched him snoring heavily. Rosie left him to sleep off the rest of the drink. The bar was closed up. No staff were visible.

Now, inside The Thatch, Rosie took the opportunity to dig around and discover more. First, she quickly looked along the hallway between the bar area and the little mini newsagents on the opposite side. As usual, piles of newspapers littered the hallway floor, but a few caught her eye; large angular holes were cut out of the paper. Rosie clocked the significance of this and moved towards the stairs, scanning a ledge along the wall that served as an area for letters and bills. An envelope with a foreign stamp caught her eye. Without hesitation, she stuffed it quickly into the oversized handbag carried in the crook of her arm.

Rosie caught Ziggy's eye, 'Possible evidence.' Ziggy was looking at her with a questioning expression. 'We'll check it when we get home; if it's unimportant, I'll pop it back.' Seemingly mollified, Ziggy trotted ahead of her up the stairs. Leading the way, he sniffed around at the edge of a door. The door slowly creaked open a crack. Sorcha glanced around, a worried, distrustful expression on her face.

'Sorcha, how are you doing?' Rosie beamed as if it was the most natural thing in the world to be snooping around her house. Sorcha fixed her eyes on Rosie with a sudden flash of recognition and stepped back from the door, leaving it open. Ziggy rushed and shot in like a bullet. He scurried around the floor, nose to the dusty-looking carpet, looking urgent and excited. Sorcha watched him with mild interest and a girlish smile.

Ziggy scampered around the room, did a couple of loops, and then shot off downstairs. Rosie watched him, feeling somewhat bemused. Sorcha had watched Ziggy's frenzied movements with a slightly detached expression and then slowly and wordlessly got back into bed, pulled the covers over herself, rolled onto her side, and closed her eyes. She seemed exhausted by the brief but hectic visit from Rosie and her nosey, canine sidekick.

Rosie followed Ziggy downstairs and shushed him as he sat barking and yelping up at the bag of golf clubs sitting behind the stairs in the hallway downstairs.

Meanwhile, back at the church, the congregation had been reeling from the shock of Jim's behaviour and what it all meant. After Jim's outburst and subsequent removal, Father Gerard had sat down on a chair at the side of the altar, used by the priest during Mass for moments of reflection, and a few tense minutes passed. An intense silence descended on the gathering; the only discernible sound was the clock ticking. Eventually, Father Gerard got up to his feet and approached the front of the altar. The flock waited expectantly for what their shepherd had to say.

'Dear brothers and sisters, I need to remind you that today we are here to pray for the soul of Sean and bid him farewell from this life. I am aware that you are probably shocked and disturbed by the behaviour of Jim, Sean's cousin. I would ask you to look at his words and actions with compassion. In fact, look at all in this community with compassion. Not least compassion for me and those Jim referred to. Today, I stand before you as your pastor and priest. I have tried to fulfil my priestly duties for the past three decades and more. But before I became a priest, I was a young man who had a romance with a young woman in the parish. This is what Jim Noonan is referring to. It is a part of my life that is now over. I can only speak for myself, and I would ask you to respect the privacy of other parties involved.' And with that admission, Father Gerard sat back down for a moment before recommencing his priestly duty of officiating at the day's sacramental occasion.

Sean's funeral passed off without further incident.

Few locals would have noticed Miss McGrath approaching Deirdre and Marie, who were walking together. After a few words with Deirdre to express her sympathy, Miss McGrath asked to speak with Marie alone. The two women, one older and a stalwart of the community, the other younger and a recent arrival, followed behind the mourners.

Sean's life in Erin's Glen had ended, but Marie felt that her life in this charming valley was now just beginning.

Chapter Thirty-Four

M.A.M

While Rosie was busy with Jim Noonan and her discoveries at The Thatch, Mairead McGrath had returned to the bookshop with Marie. Of course, Father Gerard had acknowledged Jim Noonan's outburst in the church during Sean's funeral, but many of the locals present were somewhat perplexed by the details of the accusations. Many theories were forming in the minds of those present, but few knew the whole truth. One person who was more deeply shocked than anyone was Marie herself, and Mairead understood this.

As Mairead approached Marie after the service, Marie caught sight of a familiar item of jewellery. The necklace had the heart of Celtic design and the initials M.A.M. It was an identical necklace to the one she had found in the envelope from Angel Hill and the one she wore today. She put her hand up to her neck nervously. This was why she had come to Erin's Glen, to find her mother, and that moment had now arrived.

After years working as a head teacher, Mairead was adept at masking her emotions if needed, but today, she let the tears run down her cheeks as she approached her little girl. The little girl she felt compelled to hand over all those years ago. Encouraged by the emotion in the older woman's face, Marie approached her mother, and the two embraced. A few locals looked puzzled but maintained a respectful distance as they passed by.

When Marie stepped away and looked at her mother, Mairead voiced the very thought Marie had in her mind, 'This is a dream come true.' Mairead carried on, 'I often wondered if you would come looking for me. I looked for you, but they never told me where you were. I am so, so sorry for letting you go.'

The women embraced again and then linked arms and walked along in silence.

'Come back to my flat for tea; we can talk privately there.' Marie glanced around, conscious of familiar faces looking at them both. Mary Jo was a little way behind walking on her own. The nun caught Marie's eye and smiled warmly. She raised her hand to acknowledge them both and maintained an uncharacteristically slow pace some distance behind them.

'I'm immensely proud of you. It's amazing what you have done. You've tracked me down even though I couldn't find you, and you've established a business in the town. A business that is thriving, and the shop looks beautiful.' Mairead looked ahead at Marie's shop just as it came into view.

Marie was quiet on the way back, and Mairead respected this. She had much to take in, not least that her father was an ordained priest. Mairead would have to go and talk with him later; she had some explaining to do.

The shop door had a 'closed' sign up, and Marie didn't bother turning it to 'open'. She had more important matters to attend to, like getting to know her mother.

Once upstairs in her flat and settled with tea and biscuits, Marie asked, 'Why did you never tell Father Gerard about your pregnancy?' Marie felt very odd speaking about these matters. She wasn't quite sure how to address Father Gerard now that she was aware of his relationship to her, so she decided to stay with his usual form of address.

'Well, we only had a brief relationship and were both incredibly young. When I found out I was expecting, he had broken the news that he wanted to go to the seminary to train to be a priest. He probably would have insisted on us getting married if I told him. I didn't want that. I didn't want to stand in his way if he had a vocation. So, I said nothing and let him go.'

After a long time of wondering what the truth was, Marie kept nodding, listening attentively to the answers she needed to hear.

'Back in those days, single mothers had no choice. It's not like nowadays. I had much pressure put on me to give you up. I had done well at school, and my parents had made sacrifices for my education. They wanted me to train as a teacher, and I felt guilty about letting them down. I was only seventeen years old.' At this, Mairead broke down in tears. Usually so reserved and composed, decades of grief, guilt and regret spilt out.

Marie and Mairead hugged; both had been hurt and suffered due to their separation. Marie was deeply grateful that they had made contact at last. Her mother was a sensitive, caring and much-respected figure in the community, and Marie was proud to be her daughter.

As Mairead wiped away her tears, she apologised, 'I'm sorry, Marie, look at me full of self-pity. What about you? Tell me about the people who adopted you. Please, God, they treated you well.' Mairead looked at her anxiously.

'Yes, they were good people. Both passed away now. They were lovely. I was their only child, much loved, I know, and I had everything I needed. You don't need to worry about that. But it was just…'

Marie looked off into the distance, trying to find the words.

'It was just that I never felt like I belonged with them. I always felt different. I only found out a couple of years ago that I had been adopted, and strangely, it wasn't really a shock.'

'Thank God they treated you well, anyway.' Mairead looked exhausted by all the emotions of the day. 'I'll get off soon and leave you in peace. We can catch up again in a couple of days. We'll take things easy. I know you have many questions. You can ask me anything. There have been too many secrets; it's time for the truth now.'

'Before you go, tell me about the necklace.' Marie was looking at the necklace around Mairead's neck.

Mairead smiled, 'Ah, I'm so glad you still have yours. It was the only thing they let me leave with you. Well, we shared the same initials: you are Marie Anne, and I am Mairead Aine; of course, you had my surname, McGrath. As coincidence would have it, the Miller family adopted you, so you still have the same initials.'

Marie nodded, and her mother continued, 'The heart is a Celtic infinity symbol to show that I would always love you, even if we were apart. It broke my heart to let you go.' Mairead took a deep breath and composed herself, dabbing away the tears.

The bright sunshine of the spring day had now faded, and the evening was drawing in. Marie shivered as the nighttime chill started to move in. Their time together had flown by.

'I need to go now; let you get yourself sorted for the evening, but we will talk again soon.' Mairead smiled again, looking happier than she had in a long time.

They hugged at the door, and just as Marie's mother was leaving, Deirdre was approaching the shop, Mary Jo behind her.

Marie smiled to herself; no longer was she the incomer. Now, she felt like she belonged here in Erin's Glen.

Chapter Thirty-Five

Rosie in a Jam

Earlier that afternoon, Rosie stood somewhat uncertainly in the hall of The Thatch, not sure what to do next. Ziggy had calmed down and was looking at her with a triumphant gleam in his eye.

'What?' Rosie looked at Ziggy enquiringly.

Ziggy kept her gaze for a second, then glanced back meaningfully at the bag of clubs. Rosie could hear Jim mumbling to himself. Ziggy's barks had roused Jim from his heavy slumbers. She needed to move quickly.

Without further hesitation, Rosie dived into the pockets of the golf bag. She was just about able to squeeze her slim hands and arms into the recesses of the bag. Craning her neck and peering down into the bag's depths, she lifted out clubs and inspected what was below them. Something glittered deep down in the bag. She slipped her arm right down and retrieved it; she gasped in shock to see it was bloodied. Without a second thought, Rosie threw it into her capacious handbag and had just snapped it shut when—

'What the hell do you think you are doing?'

Jim towered above her, filling the hall and bar doorway. His bulk shut out what little light was in the late afternoon's gloom.

Rosie, not usually lost for words, opened and closed her mouth. She could smell the alcohol on Jim's breath. Her own breathing was light and shallow. Jim had a volatile temper at the best of times; his sunny demeanour could quickly transpose mercury-like into sullen anger or worse. Rosie gulped. This was not looking good.

Just then, Dan ran in from the street; he had reinforcements from his boss, a burly man in his forties who looked more than a match for the unsteady Jim.

Dan and Sergeant Kennedy quickly assessed the situation. Without a word to Rosie, they each took Jim by the arm, either side and marched him towards their police car waiting outside, Jim stumbling and asking incoherent questions.

Once he was safely stowed in the car, Ziggy and Rosie stepped onto the street to observe the scene.

Dan was making a call on his mobile for an ambulance. He spoke briefly with the local operator, informing them about Sorcha, who had been left alone by her inebriated husband. He glanced at Jim sitting handcuffed in the police car, under the watchful eye of Sergeant Kennedy. When Dan finished his call, he looked at the amateur sleuth clutching her handbag.

'You get off home, Rosie. We'll wait here for the ambulance. His lordship isn't going anywhere without us!' Dan cocked his head over towards the police car. Jim sat looking stupefied and ashamed in the backseat behind a grill separating him from Sergeant Kennedy.

'Oh, Dan! I need to give you something!' Rosie offered him her handbag. He looked at her without comprehension.

'I've taken out my purse and keys; you'll be interested in what's in there.' And with that, she patted him on the arm and handed him the sizeable green leather handbag with the giant clasp. He took it somewhat uncertainly, opened it and peered inside. His expression changed. He snapped the bag shut and looked over again at Jim. Dan stroked his chin thoughtfully, shrugged his shoulders and carried on to the vehicle, carrying the handbag.

'Thanks, Rosie,' he called back.

'Oh Dan, how did you know to come over?' Rosie queried before he stepped into the car.

'You rang me!'

Rosie looked confused. 'I didn't ring you!'

'Well, it was a call from that mobile phone of yours. I recognised the number. I saw you drive earlier from the church with Jim, and then your Mini was outside The Thatch, so I knew you must have been in here.' Dan opened the bag and saw the mobile phone at the bottom. 'You must have pressed the call button when you threw this lump of a thing in! You ninny! I'll get it back to you later.' Despite the gravity of the situation, Dan smiled.

'Ah, you can keep the blessed thing,' Rosie mumbled under her breath as she walked towards her car.

A sense of frustration swept over Rosie. The police officers would see the incriminating trophy and a thick wodge of letters in her bag. They would see the obvious connection with Jim, but there was more to this. She felt the urge to discuss the situation further. But for now, Rosie decided to go home, calm down with a cup of tea and get on to the guards later. Jim was certainly no innocent anyway.

Rosie was aware of a few faces looking out from behind their lace curtains or peering around window displays from the shops on the street. Slightly embarrassed by the attention and feeling somewhat naked without her handbag on her arm, Rosie and Ziggy hopped into the Mini and zoomed off up the road.

Wait till Mary Jo hears all about this, Rosie thought with some glee.

Chapter Thirty-Six

Tying Up Loose Ends

After Rosie had driven home rather shakily and had a fortifying cup of tea, she mulled over the day's events. She was just about to phone Mary Jo when she decided to make the short journey back down to the police station, Ziggy by her side. What was on her mind couldn't wait, and she knew her friend would understand when she explained the situation later.

Ziggy trotted to the front door with her.

'Sorry, Ziggy, I need to do this alone.' She patted her furry pal on the head, and he sloped off to his basket. She straightened up, pulled her coat back into shape and looked around for her handbag. With a jolt, she remembered it would be at the station – all the more reason to get back down there. The situation's urgency propelled her out the door and into her Mini.

On the short car journey back to the station, Rosie could almost hear her heart thudding in her chest above the throaty grumble that was the customary engine noise the little car spluttered out. Her hands shook slightly as she changed gears, her nerves frayed by the heightened drama of the day's events and her anger at the police officers' complacency.

Rosie pulled up in the Mini outside the doors of the police station. She was about to get out of the car when she saw Mrs Blaney's bulky silhouette in the doorway. Dan was evidently seeing her off. She pulled her coat around her and kept her head down as she passed Rosie. But Rosie had no time to ponder on why Mrs Blaney had been in to see the police. She sprang out of the Mini and sprinted up to the police station doors.

Dan was unsurprised to see her and stepped aside as she rushed into the hallway.

'No doubt your back for your handbag,' he quipped.

'I'm back to tell you, I think you've got it all wrong,' Rosie retorted. 'I need to speak with you and your sergeant.'

Dan asked her to follow him and took her into a small office, sitting behind a large desk with Seargent Kennedy by his side, pencil poised, making notes. He looked up, a bemused and condescending smile on his face. Rosie glared at him, stony-faced and resolute in her determination to get him to see the truth. He was about to open his mouth when Rosie unceremoniously blurted out, 'It's not him.'

'What do you mean, Miss O'Reilly?' Sergeant Kennedy enquired with a note of irritation. He wanted this case wrapped up, and it was apparent to him that Jim Noonan had killed Sean.

'For goodness's sake, call me Rosie; everyone else does. And I'm telling you, Jim Noonan did not kill Sean. I'm not saying he's squeaky clean, but he's not a murderer.'

Dan, unsure how much he should divulge about the case to Rosie in front of his superior, laid out just the bare facts of the investigation so far.

'Rosie,' Dan began with much more patience and respect than his superior. Rosie turned to him with her features set into a grim expression.

'Now, Rosie,' Dan began again, trying to appease the irate sleuth. 'We...' At this, Rosie flashed her eyes at him from behind her glasses, glaring at him. 'Sorry, *you* found the blunt object that killed Sean. We have faxed a photograph of it to the pathologist, who agrees that the base's shape is consistent with the wound on Sean's head.' Dan pointed to Jim's heavy golf trophy covered in a clear plastic evidence bag on the desk. 'Also, we found a letter in the handbag from Will to Jim. It would seem Will is very much alive. Apparently, he was ready to set Jim up in a bar abroad to start a new life in the sunshine. We've made a few enquiries, and it seems Will had an insurance scam with Jim Noonan. So, you are correct. Jim is definitely not squeaky clean.'

Dan glanced at his boss, who nodded for Dan to continue.

'You will remember that The Thatch burnt down?' Rosie nodded. It was now a bit of a joke with the locals that the rebuilt Thatch had a slate roof. At the time, some banter was around about proposed new names such as Erin's Embers or The Cosy Fireside. But it had remained The Thatch despite its incongruous roof.

'Well, Will held the insurance policy and got the payout. It would seem Jim returned the favour for Will's old car workshop; Jim got the payout when that burnt down a few years after The Thatch. Sean got wind of this and wasn't going to let it go. We have witnesses that saw Sean and Jim argue, and it was getting physical.'

Rosie was nodding quickly; she could see where this was going.

'So, you think it was simply a case of Jim wanting Sean out of the picture? In case he ruined his plans to enjoy the spoils of the fraud?'

'Of course, it all ties up.' Sergeant Kennedy stood up, a satisfied expression on his face. 'We think Katie, the barmaid, was in on it. She has recently admitted that she lied about locking up that night. She has since left Erin's Glen, but we are onto the guards nationally to find out where she is. Thanks for your input, Miss. O'Reilly. I mean, Rosie. If you give your statement to my colleague here, we'll get this all sorted.'

Rosie O'Reilly was not to be dismissed so easily. Rosie stood up, and although her five-foot-nothing stature was no match for the six-footer policeman, she pulled herself up to her full height. Mirroring his calm, polite tone, she rebutted his dismissal, listing some of the facts as she saw them.

'Jim Noonan was stranded in the snow at a trade fair thirty miles away the night Sean died.'

Sergeant Kennedy sat down heavily and sighed. He wasn't going to shake off Rosie O'Reilly that easily; 'Yes, but he could have driven back in his four-by-four, bashed Sean over the head and driven back to the hotel. No one would have been none the wiser.'

Rosie listened with raised eyebrows and pursed lips. 'Well, I've asked a few questions myself at the hotel, and apparently, Jim Noonan had a few too many whiskies, and the staff had to help him up the stairs to bed. He couldn't walk, never mind drive a sixty-mile round trip in heavy snow. He'd have killed himself in that, never mind anyone else!'

Seargent Kennedy shrugged. 'Jim could have been faking it to cover himself.'

Rosie was unwilling to let go so quickly. 'And another thing. Why would he use his trophy to hit Sean? And hide it in his golf bag? He didn't make much effort to get rid of the murder weapon! It's preposterous!'

In exasperation, Rosie's voice had risen to an almost screeching pitch. Realising she was losing her cool, Rosie took a deep breath and collected herself. 'I take it all the forensic evidence has been conclusive?' Rosie asked cooly.

The officers glanced at each other.

'Err. Not yet...' The sergeant didn't finish.

Dan took the initiative and jumped in. 'We do have other definite lines of enquiry, Rosie, so rest assured we will be following those up this evening. In fact, we need to get off to do just that. We have had information about a young man in the town who might well be in the frame.'

'Right, well then, we'll see what that brings, shall we?' And with that, Rosie spun on her heel and was out the door.

'Rosie!' Dan called out after her.

'What?' she snapped back at him.

'Your handbag.'

Usually polite and good-natured, Rosie grabbed it off him and squeezed out, 'Thank you,' with much less graciousness than usual. 'I'll be back.' And with that, Rosie O'Reilly nestled her empty handbag into the crook of her arm, straightened her coat, and, with her head held high, walked out of the door of the police station.

Chapter Thirty-Seven

From the Mouths of Babes

Trish O'Hara had attended Sean's funeral along with her husband Seamus. Sean and Seamus had known each other at school but had gone their separate ways after Sean's father, Will, had disappeared. Sean had become moody and withdrawn; he had started to drink heavily. Seamus had his own little family to take care of, so he let the friendship drift.

That day, his little daughter, Roisin, was in school when all the drama at the church had unfolded. Her parents were glad she had not witnessed Jim's bizarre behaviour and had picked her up from school later that day, as usual. Had she been at the funeral, Trish dreaded the questions Roisin might have asked. Trish had resisted the urge to talk about the day's events to any neighbours, who understood the subject was best not broached in front of the child.

Despite the odd day that it had been, Trish had to get on with the usual chores and errands. She had closed up her hair and beauty salon that day as a mark of respect to Seans's passing. She hadn't known him well, and he was not well-liked by all accounts, but she felt it was important to show some respect. Many shops were closed, and although Rainbow Row looked cheerful in the incipient spring sunshine, the street had a sombre atmosphere that day. The early brightness had given way to a dull, cloudy afternoon, and the last dregs of winter darkness closed in early that afternoon.

Seamus was downstairs, out the back in his workshop, tinkering with the engine on his motorcycle. He usually did this when he felt unsettled or worried, and today was an unsettling day for many in Erin's Glen.

Roisin and Trish sat upstairs in the living room of their flat above the hair salon. Trish had prepared a stew for dinner, and she could hear it gently bubbling away in the kitchen that was visible to her in their open-plan living space. The room was quiet except for the ticking of a clock, the odd crackle and pop from the wood burner and Roisin's humming as she brushed the hair of Sandra, her beloved doll with the long purple hair.

Looking at her magazine, *Irish Hair Weekly*, Trish was grateful to have a few minutes of peace. Trish thought it was important that she kept up to date with changing trends. With a mug of tea on the little table by her side, Trish felt more relaxed than she had in quite a while. She had been unsettled by Sean's death but had comforted herself with the mistaken belief that he had slipped and fallen in the snow and was overcome by hypothermia. She convinced herself that the experts had got it wrong. This was easier for her to accept than thinking someone had been murdered just across the road from her home and business. It was not a comforting thought to think that poor young fellow lay there on his own and died, but it was preferable to thinking there was a murderer out there. With these preoccupations, she got up and looked out the window.

The street outside was silent in the dying light of the day. The shops were all closed up. There was a light on over in The Thatch, but all the curtains were closed. Trish craned her head round to look further up the street. A police car was parked a little way up. But that could mean anything; she reassured herself, probably one of the guards out getting their fish and chip supper. She closed her curtains and returned to the comforting sight of her familiar living room. A low lamp and a warm glow from the wood burner in the corner of the room dimly lit the room.

Trish caught sight of Roisin, who had been looking at her sheepishly.

'You all right, Munchkin?' her mother enquired, ruffling her hair as she drew closer to her daughter.

Roisin nodded and went back to brushing her doll's hair. Trish sighed, shaking off a vague sense of disquiet, and sat in the armchair opposite, tucking her legs under her, and resumed looking at her magazine.

Roisin wriggled to the edge of the sofa she was sitting on and peered across at the magazine her mother was reading. Roisin, keen to show her developing reading skills, read the title to her mother.

Trish looked up and smiled, 'Clever girl!'

Roisin slipped off the sofa and approached her mother for a hug. Trish sat forward in the armchair and opened her arms to her daughter. With a mother's intuition, Trish sensed something was on her daughter's mind. She pulled Roisin onto her lap and watched closely as Roisin continued brushing her doll's hair. A shadow seemed to have been cast over her childish features. Keeping her eyes cast downwards, fixed on her task, her little chin started to tremble. She looked up and gave Trish a worried glance.

Trish suddenly felt alarmed. Her daughter was usually a bright and vivacious girl, and this sombre behaviour was not in keeping with her usual demeanour.

With a thudding heart, Trish cupped Roisin's chin in her hand and tilted her face to look up at her, 'What is it?'

Holding Roisin on her lap, she could feel her slight frame tense. Trish felt increasingly disturbed by her daughter's behaviour.

'Mammy…'

'Yes, darlin', what is it?'

'Mammy, don't be cross with me.'

Trish, desperate to discover what was bothering her little girl, promised she would not get cross. Trish was trying extremely hard not to let the rising panic take over.

'Is it someone at school? Is someone bullying you?'

Roisin briefly shook her head and continued brushing her doll's hair, keeping her eyes fixed on it.

'Mammy, it's about that man across the road.'

'Which man?'

'Now, Mammy, don't be getting cross; I know you told me not to look out at people or be nosey, but…'

Roisin trailed off. She seemed to be losing the courage to tell her mother the problem.

'But what, Roisin? I promise you I won't get angry, but if something is worrying you, it's best to talk to me about it. Then we can sort it out, whatever it is.'

'Well, I was just thinking. I heard you and Daddy talking about that man. That man he used to be friends with. The one that died.'

Trish hadn't been aware of talking about Sean that day in Roisin's hearing, but she did tend to hang around by the door listening to conversations. Trish had talked to Roisin about this before and told her off about it. The irritation that Trish had promised she would not show was starting to creep up. She knew her daughter's curiosity would get the best of her someday. The worry and panic that Trish had felt about what Roisin would share was now turning to anger. Seeing a red flush creep up her mother's neck, Roisin started losing her nerve. Trish quickly reassured her, 'It's all right, Roisin, just tell Mammy what it is that's bothering you.'

'Well, some people at school were talking about that man, saying he wasn't very nice.'

'Okay...' Trish wasn't sure where this conversation was heading, but she kept her calm, on edge to find out what Roisin wanted to share. It was obviously something that had been playing on her mind.

'Well, I didn't say anything about what I saw before because I thought he was a bad man.'

'Say what, darling?' Trish prompted.

'And I thought you might get cross with me.'

Trish nearly hissed the words through gritted teeth, but she smiled sweetly and murmured, 'I'm not cross.'

Roisin curled the doll's long trailing hair around her fingers. 'Well, I saw someone hit the man, and he fell. I think it was the man who died.'

Trish was horrified that her young daughter could have witnessed such an incident. 'Are you sure? Maybe it was just a dream? Maybe your mind is just playing tricks on you?' Trish looked at Roisin, her brows furrowed with concern and disbelief.

'I'm sure, I saw it, Mammy. It was that night of the snow. I was looking out at the snow because it looked so pretty. I wasn't snooping, honest. I was so worried I'd done wrong by being nosey I didn't tell you, and then when all the boys and girls at school said he was an evil man and it was a good job he was gone. Miss Mulligan told me off for making up tales, but it's true, Mammy! I didn't know what to say or who to tell. I'm so sorry for being nosey!' And with that, Roisin burst into fits of tears. Many days and nights of tears and tension were unleashed as Trish held her daughter in her arms.

Just then, there was a loud knock on the door.

Chapter Thirty-Eight

Nun on the Run

Shortly after Rosie's motor had rumbled down the street on the journey home, Mary Jo made her way swiftly down past Rainbow Row. Despite all the recent disturbing events in town, the occupants of Erin's Glen were making their annual efforts to spruce the place up for the next big date on the Erin's Glen calendar.

Mary Jo took some comfort from these signs of normality and was also lulled by the soft thud, thud of her feet on the pavement as she jogged steadily, her breath coming and going rapidly, distracted by her appreciation of the town's decorations and her own thoughts.

'Huh! Oh sister, sorry.' A distraught-looking Trish O'Hara looked up at Mary Jo. She had been rushing along, head down, her brow furrowed in concern and literally bumped into the nun who was looking elsewhere. Both reeled in shock, jolted by the impact.

'Oh, that's me, not looking where I am going,' Mary Jo apologised in turn and stopped short, looking into Trish's eyes and taking in the look of worry on Trish's face. 'What is it, love?'

'Oh, Sister.' Tears came into Trish's eyes. 'It's all such a mess…' Trish was sobbing now. 'The guards have taken in my Seamus. He's over there now, and to make matters worse, my wee girl has seen something terrible, and I need to speak with the police. They wouldn't listen to me when they were taking Seamus. They told me to come over to the station and make a statement. I'm on my way there now. But I need to be quick; Kay is keeping an eye on Roisin for me, and I'll need to get back… I'll talk to you again.' Trish's voice trailed off as she trotted off up the street.

Just then, Deirdre was across the road. Mary Jo could see her well enough to register the relaxed look on her face as she made her way down the street. She raised a hand in greeting, smiling at Mary Jo and waiting while the nun crossed the road to speak to the younger woman.

'How are you doing?' Mary Jo swooped Deirdre up in a hug and stroked her shoulder as she responded. The nun was trying hard to shake off her distress at Trish's news and focus on Deirdre's newfound contentment.

'Ach, I'm doing well, sister. I'm putting all that business behind me, and I've decided to get on with my life and make the best of things.'

'Right so,' Mary Jo nodded decisively, smiling with approval.

'I'm just popping in to see Marie.' Just as Deirdre shared this piece of information, Mary Jo saw Mairead McGrath emerge from the shop. Marie behind her.

'Hello, ladies,' Mairead McGrath greeted Mary Jo and Deirdre with her customary warm smile. 'How are you doing?'

'Just grand,' Mary Jo confirmed. 'Well, I'd best be getting on. I've got evening prayers with the sisters, and it's my turn to do the dinner. I'll be seeing you!' She waved at her friends, and as she glanced back, she saw Deirdre hugging Marie and disappearing into the bookshop.

'Well, it's all going on this evening,' she murmured to herself as she trotted up the road back to the warmth of Riverside House.

Later that same evening, the two officers emerged from the station and ambled down the road towards Mrs Blaney's B&B. They had received notification from the labs about material found on the murder weapon.

To further confound their wish to get the case all wrapped up, Trish O Hara had been in to see them. There was no getting away from it; they needed to question their assumptions and get back to the drawing board. The whole case might now hinge on Mrs Blaney's housekeeping skills or, rather, the lack of them.

With any luck.

....

The police officers sat at their desks later that night, weighing up the evidence garnered that day. In truth, they felt weary from all the twists and turns the day had brought. Sergeant Kennedy had been on the phone to grovel an apology to his wife, expecting him home for an anniversary dinner. He still felt disgruntled about Rosie's interference as he saw it. Just then, the phone rang, sounding louder than usual in the quiet of the night.

Dan answered. He listened to the caller for just a few seconds and then handed the phone to his superior.

'It's for you. It's Rosie O'Reilly; she's just remembered something from way back and reckons she knows exactly who killed Sean.'

Chapter Thirty-Nine

All's Well That Ends Well

Mary Jo and Rosie sat in her spacious kitchen at Rosie's big pine table. The spring sunshine poured in, and Ziggy softly snored in his basket by the range.

They had the local paper spread out on the table.

Local Publican Tried for Fraud and Blackmail

Both women tutted over their tea.

'Well, it's a good thing you had your eyes open, Rosie, you put them straight; otherwise, that poor sinner would be up for murder.' Mary Jo shook her head; despite Jim's misdeeds, she had compassion for this weak man tempted by the promise of a better life in the sunshine.

'Yes indeed,' Rosie agreed with just a hint of self-satisfaction.

'It was all in here.' Rosie tapped her head. 'I remember that evening she bumped into me outside The Thatch. It stuck in my head. I had a feeling she was up to no good, and her name rang a bell... Isabella

Santos. We don't get many of them around here, but I knew I had seen it somewhere before.'

Rosie was referring to the mysterious guest at Mrs Blaney's B&B. Her eagle eye and reliable memory had served her well and ensured justice was done.

'I remembered seeing that name in the register for baptisms in our parish record book. It was a bit before my time, but it was there, an entry for 17th March 1951. I checked with old Mrs Kilpatrick at the post office; she was extremely helpful. She remembered the Spanish lady over at Will's back in the late '40s. It's a team effort, you know.' Rosie patted Mary Jo on the arm with a smile. Ziggy looked up from his slumbers as if in agreement.

Rosie continued, 'It also helped that that wee girl, Roisin, could identify Isabella. She's a wee dote, that child and bright as a button! But what a carry-on her daddy being taken in for questioning! Seamus had been out at a support meeting to keep himself sober! That's why he had broken off his friendship with Sean all those years ago; Sean was too fond of the sauce and was getting Seamus into trouble. It was bad luck that Seamus was out the night Sean got murdered.'

'Well, it was a blessing that a few others at the meeting were willing to speak up for him. They let the guards know he was with them and left far too early to be a suspect. Silly eegits in uniforms!' Usually respectful of authority, Mary Jo dismissed the guards with a contemptuous laugh.

She became more serious when she reflected on the anxiety the lack of police competence had caused Trish and Roisin. 'Imagine them saying the wee girl had made up her story to protect her father.'

Both women tutted. The sight of the lady with the long black hair bludgeoning Sean until he fell in the street had played on Roisin's mind for weeks. It took much courage for her to speak up. It was true that the police had quickly dismissed her testimony as a childish attempt to take the focus off her father.

'You know what tickled me about the outcome?' Rosie glanced at Mary Jo, hoping she would see the lighter side too. 'The culprit was right under the nose of that biddy Mrs Blaney, and she never suspected a thing! She was insinuating that Seamus was involved way back when it first happened. You know, I think it was Mrs Blaney who tipped off the police and put them on the wrong track. Little did she know she was harbouring the true criminal!'

Mary Jo indulged her friend with a wry smile and a shake of her head.

Rosie loved retelling the tale that unravelled the mystery and was keen to recount the story. Mary Jo, a kind and patient woman, humoured her and continued to listen, even though she knew every twist and turn of the tale.

'That old Will was quite a dark horse. As well as getting inveigled into all that insurance scam business, he had secrets that went way back. He had kept that daughter, Isabella, a secret. Aye, the mother was Ricarda, a Spanish lady who had stayed on here after the war. My mother thought he was involved with her, but it was all hushed up. I remembered her telling me about it, but you know how Mammy was; she was always chatting on about something or other, and I had forgotten all about it. She told me that at the time, Will said Ricarda was lodging with him and working in the bar. But it would seem that she fell pregnant by him. After she found out she was expecting, he kept her upstairs and told people she had already left. Then he smuggled her and the baby out of Erin's Glen. But no one knew that before she left Erin's Glen, Ricarda had the baby baptised in secret before taking her back to Spain. So that's how Isabella's name was in the parish records.'

'So, you took this information to that lazy so-and-so Kennedy, and that prompted the peelers into digging around.' Mary's compassion didn't extend to police officers who weren't doing their jobs properly.

Rosie laughed, 'Yes, it's just as well. Mrs Blaney wasn't too quick cleaning the rooms at her B&B. Of course, she blamed Katie! She's been complaining about Katie just taking off like that.'

Mary Jo looked concerned. 'So what happened to Katie? She just disappeared after all that business with Sean?'

Rosie was quick to answer, 'She's with her aunt in Dublin. She couldn't face all the gossip in the town. She lied to the police. The police have been in touch with her, of course. Apparently, Katie had left the door to The Thatch open that night Sean was killed; she was expecting a visit from Sean. Poor Deirdre, he was carrying on with Katie behind her back.' Rosie tutted. 'Anyway, the open door gave Isabella the opportunity to drop the trophy into Jim's bag quickly. She had stolen the trophy from the bar and had it in her bag, just waiting for an opportunity to clobber Sean. That was something else that had been playing in the back of my mind – I had seen Isabella come outside the bar looking furtive; that must have been when she took the trophy. Of course, she then planted the evidence on Jim. What sealed it was the forensics. Isabella had wiped her prints, but a tiny dark hair stuck to the trophy matched the hair found on the pillowcase used by Isabella Santos at the B&B. Her beautiful, long, dark hair was her undoing. Of course, by the time those lazy so-and-sos realised what was going on, Miss Santos had fled, but thanks to Interpol and the Spanish police, she'll be on her way back to face the music.' Rosie paused to savour justice being done. 'Isabella's real name on her passport is Elizabeth Patricia Santos Flynn. She didn't want locals to link her with Will Flynn, so she used a variation of her name. Unfortunately for her,

Isabella, the Spanish for Elizabeth, matched the record of her baptism. It would seem that even she didn't know about the baptism herself.'

Mary Jo continued, picking up where Rosie left off, 'Aye, the Spanish police confirmed Will was alive and has been living with Ricarda, Isabella's mother, all these years. I heard he is in a hospice. He was in touch with Jim, and a lot of money was coming Jim's way from all the scams, Sean too, apparently. I suppose Isabella was unhappy about sharing her inheritance. I think he had sent Isabella to scout what was happening in the old place. I don't think he would want to kill his own kith and kin.'

'But Isabella decided to take matters into her own hands and do Sean in. Imagine that, her half-brother? Her flesh and blood.' Rosie shook her head. 'Staging it to look like Jim was the perpetrator killed two birds with one stone, so to speak. Of course, it didn't look good for Jim as he was in communication with old Will – there were all those letters from Will, so Jim had dug a bit of a hole for himself.'

Mary Jo considered Isabella's shocking modus operandi further, 'So get rid of Sean and pin the blame on Sean's cousin, so he'd be out of the picture, behind bars. She had a go at pushing Deirdre into the river that morning, too. Apparently, she was worried Deirdre would claim the inheritance as Sean's wife. Isabella assumed they were married.'

Both women shook their heads sadly, dumbfounded by the depths humanity could sink to. All for the love of money.

'For the love of money is the root of all evil: while some coveted after, they have erred from the faith and pierced themselves through with many sorrows.'

Rosie looked at Mary Jo, who had just quoted the scripture. 'Right so,' she agreed as she surveyed her faithful friend. Rosie made allowances as Mary Jo *was* a nun, after all. She couldn't help but get all religious on her sometimes.

They both sipped their tea contemplatively. Rosie broke the silence, 'Poor Marie, at first, she thought Will might have been her father. That's why she was so disturbed by Sean's death, thinking he was her half-brother. Ah well, it's lovely that Marie has got to know her mammy and daddy. Although it will take some getting used to Father being a father if you know what I mean!'

Both ladies giggled at the little joke and looked out at the sunshine and showers that had produced a stunning rainbow over the hills surrounding Erin's Glen.

'Right, well, I'd best be getting on. We've got the last craft group meeting tonight before the big parade next week. I need to get back and get the tea sorted and myself organised. See you later.' Mary Jo hugged her friend warmly and strode off down the road back to Riverside House.

Chapter Forty

The Big Parade

The next day, Rosie, Mary Jo, Marie, and Deirdre sat around Marie's small coffee table upstairs in her flat. The items on sale that day inside the shop were evidence of the craft group's prodigious creativity. They had worked hard the previous evening to get everything ready. The little group had produced shamrocks in various media, including quilted shamrock potholders, shamrock suncatchers, tea cosies and multiple items of clothing and household linens, all with a shamrock theme. Their many creative productions would be sold in the shop and were so numerous that they spilt out onto a stall just outside the stationers. All the proceeds would go to fund books for the school library at The Carmelite Convent of Our Lady of the Immaculate Conception Girls' School. Marie's Valentine's display had given way to a window filled with artistically draped pastel silk in the shape and hues of a rainbow, a sizeable cauldron-shaped pot, a few leprechauns, and many shamrocks.

It was still early on the morning of St Patrick's Day, and the street as yet was quiet, just a few stallholders starting to set up to take advantage of the passing trade the day's festivities would bring.

The four women had shared much over the past few eventful weeks. They had agreed to meet early this morning to enjoy a special breakfast of potato farls dripping in butter and big mugs of tea to reflect on and celebrate their achievements.

While they were chatting, drinking tea, and eating the buttery farls, Ziggy sprung up from under the table, eyes alert and ready to dart across the room. He had spotted the illusive black and white feline who had decided to give an appearance.

Rose instinctively held on to Ziggy's collar, saying his name reproachfully. He sat down resentfully, thwarted in his desire to chase the nonchalant cat who now sat blinking at him with disingenuous innocence.

'Ah, so Patch turned up then!' Mary Jo exclaimed and then, after a pause, said, 'But you have a cat, don't you, Marie? Do they get on okay?'

Marie and Deirdre looked at each other and laughed; he's called 'Willow-Patch now. It turns out he had decided to move here during all the carry-on I had at Scanlon Street.'

This arrangement had worked out fine as Willow-Patch was not the only one to move into the flat above the bookshop. Marie and Deirdre's friendship had blossomed during the difficulties of the previous few weeks, and the women had decided to expand the business to incorporate a café. Deirdre had left the unhappy home she shared with Sean and set up home in the flat with Marie.

Just then, the doorbell tinkled downstairs. 'It's only me,' Mairead McGrath's voice called up the stairs, and the women shuffled around, making room for Marie's mother. Marie hugged her warmly, and the conversation resumed, turning to the local community.

'How are you doing, Mairead? Everything all right up at the school?' Rosie was keen to know how the community had received the news about her personal life. But apparently, everyone had accepted the revelation that the local head teacher had a daughter; recent dramatic events had put her family life into the shade.

'There were a few raised eyebrows at the recent board of governors meeting, but no one said anything. I think it's been harder for Gerard. But they'll get used to it,' Mairead answered.

Marie could see the tears in her mother's eyes. She still hadn't quite come to terms with the guilt she felt about handing over her baby daughter all those years ago, but she was only seventeen at the time and had a promising career in education ahead of her. The 1950s were a hugely different time; thankfully, things had moved on in the forty years since her separation from her child. Marie was aware of this and leaned over and squeezed her mother's hand.

There was a pause in the conversation, and Mary Jo's gaze drifted out the window to The Thatch across the road. Unusually for such a busy day, it was closed up. Rosie caught her friend's gaze, 'I've heard that Sorcha is doing well. She's staying with a cousin in Rocksheelan.'

Mary Jo nodded thoughtfully.

'Right, well, we'd best be making a move.' Rosie started to gather up her belongings when suddenly they all jumped in response to a loud crash.

'Oh, Ziggy!' they all chorused in exasperation.

Ziggy had cleared all the teacups and plates off the low table with one swish of his fanned tail. The debris of broken crockery and the remains of the breakfast were on the floor.

'I'm so sorry!' Rosie apologised, aghast at the mess he had created. But there was no need to apologise as Willow-Patch enjoyed clearing up the last buttery treats off the floor. Ziggy eyed the cat resentfully as Rosie held him in check. The others scurried about picking up the breakfast things and sweeping up.

Once order was restored, the little band of ladies and pets made their way downstairs. The sound of some traditional music was starting to drift down the street as the band was getting tuned up for the big parade. Mary Jo, Rosie, Mairead, Deirdre and Marie stepped onto the road to admire the bunting and shop decorations.

'You stand there, and I'll take a photo.' Rosie produced a new Polaroid camera from her bag. 'I got myself this. I've decided to take snaps to keep as evidence if I notice anything else interesting going on around here!'

The ladies began to assemble themselves at the front of the shop under the new sign that read,

Reid and Wright.

Mairead looked up. 'Oh, I've just noticed you've got a new sign!' she commented. 'Ah, I get it – Marie, you've taken your father's surname, Reid, and of course Deirdre, your second name is Wright!'

Smiling, she stood beside her daughter as Rosie snapped the button on her new camera. They all waited with bated breath as the picture slowly slid out of the front of the camera.

An image of the four ladies came into view – four headless ladies.

'*Rosie!*' they shouted in unison.

If you enjoyed reading 'Murder in Erin's Glen,' you will love Murder in the Fairy Ring, book two in the Erin's Glen series.

Do fairies exist? Maybe they do – maybe they don't. But not many people in Ireland would risk upsetting them. Airport runways have been re-routed and building projects cancelled for fear of angering the 'little people'.

Even in 1990, the year this mystery unfolds, superstition still abounds in the idyllic country town of Erin's Glen. And when a body turns up in the local fairy ring, suspicion falls on the supernatural folk.

As shocking events shake the usually tranquil community, sleuth Rosie O'Reilly and her trusty spaniel, Ziggy, become embroiled in a baffling murder mystery. Rosie can't help but wonder if the ancient legends are more than just fairy stories.

Rosie delves deep into the heart of the enchanted Glen. But as she inches closer to the truth, she discovers that unravelling the mystery may come at a price she never imagined.

Filled with whimsy, warmth, and a sprinkle of magic, 'Murder in the Fairy Ring' is a delightful cosy crime tale. Prepare to be whisked away to the captivating landscapes of rural Ireland, where myth blurs tantalisingly with reality.

Murder in the Fairy Ring
Chapter One
Astray

The night was inky black. A thick layer of cloud obscured the stars that usually twinkled over Erin's Glen. A wispy veil of mist hovered close to the ground and seemed to be rising as the darkness closed in. Toddy lived a way out of the town and had a long walk back home to his dilapidated cottage in the woods. Half an hour earlier, he had left the Shenanigans pub in town with a gaggle of other locals. The guards were about, and the proprietor of this drinking establishment wanted to hold onto his license, so he called last orders and moved the crowd out onto the street just before 11 pm.

Toddy had begun his journey shiny-faced and bleary-eyed, still giggling and hiccupping. He had been slightly unsteady on his feet but stable enough to walk the few miles home. A few of his drinking pals called out cheery goodbyes and mild jocular insults as they went their separate ways on the road out of town. It was mid-week, and after the struggle of drinkers had dispersed, a silence had crept over the street. The shop sign for Quinn's Curiosities, the antique store on the high street, creaked in the wind that now whistled along the street. A few streetlights blinked. Toddy turned up his collar and shook his cap out of his pocket. He pulled it on over his unruly black curly hair and grimaced as the breeze picked up with a damp, chill edge to it.

'Onwards and upwards', he murmured to himself as he plodded on up the street towards the hill fort and home.

Toddy didn't relish his return to his squalid home. He had lived in the cottage all his life, and now that his parents had passed on, he was there alone. He had taken it upon himself to be an unofficial custodian of the hill fort and felt that his presence there was required to protect the ancient site. His father had told him tales of how this duty was in the family, passed on from father to son down the generations. However, the pay for this self-appointed role was non-existent, and Toddy had to make do with state handouts based on his claims of poor health, supplemented by a poached rabbit and homegrown vegetables for many of his meals. Despite his material poverty, he did have a sense of purpose and an iron-clad belief in the 'sidhe' or little people that he believed inhabited the sacred mound that he protected.

As Toddy left the environs of the town tonight, the darkness intensified. He passed the old stone that marked the entry into the town of Erin's Glen, and he glanced down at it. He could barely make it out. The mist that had been cleared along the high street by the sudden wind now started to swirl about his legs and seemed to be creeping up his body as he walked briskly along. His pace had quickened, and his gait had levelled out now that he had sobered up in the frigid night air. He looked up, expecting to see some stars as he left behind the lights of the town, but the sky was a heavy, cloudy-black dome above his head, moonless and starless. Toddy had no torch, but he wasn't too concerned; he knew the route home well. He had walked it thousands of times, first with his parents and school pals and now, as an adult, increasingly solitary. He knew he was considered an oddity in the town, but he accepted it as part of his role.

His life now had few immediate ties with the local community. The bonds that brought people together in the town, such as church, school, sports and shopping, were not a regular part of his existence. He wasn't one for 'kissing the altar gates' as his mother used to put it; he didn't go near the church. He had no family now, and due to his bad health as a child and adolescent, he played no sports. His only trip into town most weeks was to venture down to Shenanigans mid-week to take advantage of the cheap drinks. Fortified by a few

Guinness, he would latch on to a crowd there, usually hovering on the edge. He had learned the script of what to say – the usual jokes, jibes and nicknames that he and the others used every time they saw each other. It was a jovial social shorthand that obliterated the need for any proper conversation. That suited him. He didn't want any intrusive questions. But the men he exchanged banter with, the grown boys he went to school with, now had families of their own and jobs to go to. Toddy just had his cottage and his role of watcher and keeper.

As he rolled these thoughts around in his mind, familiar musings, he became conscious of the mist getting denser now as he left the town a long way behind him. He put his hand out in front of him and couldn't see it. He felt his levels of anxiety rise due to the dark closing in around him, rendering him blind as he walked home on his own. He could hear the river gushing along in the darkness and was gripped by an almost primal phobia of falling into the depths of the sub-zero water. Toddy couldn't swim, and nightmares of drowning haunted him. Bad dreams seemed to trouble him more recently, isolated as he was in his cottage at night.

Toddy lifted his feet with increased awareness as he walked on. He stamped each foot down with a sense of purpose. He could feel the road beneath his feet and hear the thud of his boots on the tarmac. The land was his home, and his intuitive closeness to the earth comforted him. With a countryman's sense of direction and knowledge of the landscape, he knew where the river was in relation to the road. 'No chance of me falling in like some townie eegit'. He comforted himself with these thoughts and concentrated on the rhythmic sound of his steps along the road.

After a few paces, he stopped.

The usual landmarks, the trees, hedges, walls, mounds of earth, and the well he looked for as his two-mile marker out of town had all disappeared. Toddy felt a wave of a vertigo-like sensation sweep over him and thought he might fall to the road. His innate sense of direction was gone. He turned around, then around again. A sick, icy panic knotted in his stomach and seeped up through his intestines into his chest and spread out into his limbs. He felt jittery and disorientated by the lack of his inner compass, which usually functioned so well. He stood in the murky, misty darkness, frozen to the spot. He was confused by the sudden disappearance of the external landmarks that he usually used as his guide.

Toddy took a breath and shook himself. He strode forward in a futile attempt to regain his confidence and sense of direction. He stopped again. Yes, he was sure of it now. He could hear a clip-clop behind him.

He stopped, and it stopped.

He walked on a few paces; there it was again.

Clip clop, clip clop.

He stopped abruptly, his body tense with fear and cold.

Silence.

He stood stationary, frozen by a sudden terror in the claustrophobic darkness. He could feel the tendrils of mist creep along his cheek like fingers. The fog surrounded him and hovered, silent and waiting as he waited. Toddy could hear his raspy breathing. In the distance, an owl hooted.

He gritted his teeth and strode on resolutely.

The clip-clop started again. It seemed to be following him; he quickened his pace, and it got quicker. Toddy ran and stumbled into the grass verge at the side of the road, unable to make out where the road ended, and the fields began. He tripped up in the thick, long grass and fell heavily into the wet foliage. His old, broken boots had let in the wet from the grass, and he swore as his feet became soggy. As he lay shivering in the grass, he could hear the hungry gushing of the river closer now. He swallowed hard. The knot of panic now wedged in his throat, he called out hoarsely, 'Who is it?'

No answer.

Chapter Two – Change in the Air

The spring sunshine splintered the bare trees. The wooded area, sheltered by a circle of green hills and the mountain in the distance, was quiet and still. A few songbirds, returned from their winter sojourn, made a distinctive chiff-chaff sound in the distance. Ziggy, a curly-haired chocolate-coloured spaniel, scampered ahead of Rosie, a neat grey-haired lady dressed in Wellington boots and a heavy tweed coat. Rosie loved mornings like this. She smiled as she tilted her head to feel the warmth of the gentle sunshine on her face.

Over the winter, these woods had often been under a blanket of snow, but now enticed by the warmth of spring, tiny emerald shoots appeared. The daffodils provided splashes of golden colour, and Rosie spotted some early bluebells. The trees, so recently bare and stark, were now adorned with unfurling green buds. A sense of awakening and renewal was in the air. After a difficult few months over the winter, Rosie's heart began to warm with a sense of hope.

A few puffy white clouds drifted across the pure blue sky. The air sparkled with a crystal-clear freshness unique to Erin's Glen. Everything felt alive, and the sunshine sparkled off the young green leaves. Rosie paused and breathed in the sharp pine scent of the wood, her fingers brushing the rough textured bark of an oak tree she was standing by.

Suddenly, her attention was drawn to the spot where Ziggy had decided to stop abruptly…

If you enjoyed this sample from Murder in the Fairy Ring, please go to: https://books2read.com/erinsglen2

You can follow the author A.P. Ryan at .facebook.com/GlensideBooks.

Printed in Great Britain
by Amazon